Readers love And

A Taste of Love

"…an emotional story that will have you in tears one minute, smiling and laughing the next."
—Love Romances & More

A Shared Range

"…another enjoyable read filled with two well rounded and likable guys."
—Literary Nymphs

Pump Me Up

"Andrew Grey is a master storyteller. His stories have heart and the characters fairly leap off the pages to completely captivate you."
—Love Romances & More

An Unexpected Vintage

"There's nothing like a story that reminds you to get out and enjoy life!"
—Fallen Angel Reviews

Love Means… Freedom

"Mr. Grey has, once again, brought to life compelling characters with whom readers can identify and about whom we can care deeply. This is one of those books best read snuggled up in a cozy, favorite chair while the wind howls outside."
—Whipped Cream Erotic Romance Reviews

http://www.dreamspinnerpress.com

Books by
Andrew Grey

The Bottled Up stories
Bottled Up
Uncorked
The Best Revenge
An Unexpected Vintage
A Shared Range

The Children of Bacchus stories
Children of Bacchus
Thursday's Child
Child of Joy

The Love Means… stories
Love Means… No Shame
Love Means… Courage
Love Means… No Boundaries
Love Means… Freedom
Love Means… No Fear

Accompanied by a Waltz
A Shared Range
A Taste of Love

All published by
Dreamspinner Press

ACCOMPANIED by a Waltz

ANDREW GREY

Dreamspinner Press

Published by
Dreamspinner Press
4760 Preston Road
Suite 244-149
Frisco, TX 75034
http://www.dreamspinnerpress.com/

This is a work of fiction. Names, characters, places, and incidents either are the product of the author's imagination or are used fictitiously, and any resemblance to actual persons, living or dead, business establishments, events, or locales is entirely coincidental.

Accompanied by a Waltz
Copyright © 2011 by Andrew Grey

Cover Art by Justin James   dare.empire@gmail.com
Cover Design by Mara McKennen

All rights reserved. No part of this book may be reproduced or transmitted in any form or by any means, electronic or mechanical, including photocopying, recording, or by any information storage and retrieval system without the written permission of the Publisher, except where permitted by law. To request permission and all other inquiries, contact Dreamspinner Press, 4760 Preston Road, Suite 244-149, Frisco, TX 75034
http://www.dreamspinnerpress.com/

ISBN: 978-1-61581-797-9

Printed in the United States of America
First Edition
February, 2011

eBook edition available
eBook ISBN: 978-1-61581-798-6

For Mom and Dad.

CHAPTER One

Two years ago

"Happy birthday!"

He cracked his eyes open to see his lover standing over him, carrying a tray and wearing nothing but a smile. "You know I hate birthdays, and turning forty-five is nothing to celebrate," Jonathon responded to Greg's cheerful voice. "What are you doing here, anyway?" he added as sleep fell away and he remembered that Greg was supposed to be in Los Angeles on business, not standing in their bedroom with breakfast in bed. Sitting up, the covers pooling in his lap, Jonathon made room on their bed.

The mattress dipped as Greg sat down, placing the tray over Jonathon's legs before slipping beneath the blankets next to his lover. "I've never missed your birthday, not in seventeen years together, and I don't intend to start now. I finished the infernal meeting yesterday and even got Harry Jenkins, the world's most persnickety actor, to sign the damned contract before catching the red-eye. I landed at Kennedy a few hours ago and drove right here."

Jonathon smiled, reaching out as Greg leaned closer, their lips touching lightly.

"Happy Birthday, Boo."

Jonathon sighed softly against those familiar and loved lips, the very private nickname Greg had for him warming his heart, just as it had for over a decade. Shortly after they met, Greg had found out that Jonathon's middle name was Beauregard, and he'd loved it. Greg had started calling him his Beau and eventually shortened it to Boo, and it had been that way ever since.

"We have lunch with the kids today, and after that I'm off for the next three days. Where would you like to go?" Greg kissed him again before leaning back against the headboard with a smile.

Jonathon looked over the breakfast tray, pulling his gaze away from Greg. He'd been so sweet; he didn't want to do anything to spoil it. "You know where I want to go," was all he said, doing his best to push the thought of lunch with Greg's three children out of his mind.

"I do, and after we finish breakfast"—Greg leaned close again, lips tugging on an ear; the sensation had Jonathon moaning again—"you can pack while I make sure everything is all set at the office. Then we can drive to the lake. I already called the service, and they said they'll have the house opened up, stocked, and ready. We won't have to leave the entire time unless we want to."

Jonathon looked up from the tray, feeling a little choked up. "Thank you," he replied softly.

"Boo." Jonathon felt a finger slide under his chin. "I understand about the kids. I had a talk with all three of them and told them that they're all adults now and it was time they started acting like it."

Greg picked up one of the berries off the plate, bringing it to Jonathon's mouth, and his lips opened automatically, sucking in the berry and one of Greg's fingers as well.

"I love you, Jonathon Pfister, and I have almost since the day we first met—and nothing is going to change that. They need to realize it and get over it." Jonathon heard Greg sigh softly. "I should have dealt with them a long time ago."

"It's not your fault, and you can't make them like me." Jonathon took a bite of egg, fluffy and light, before getting another forkful, feeding it to Greg with a slight leer. "I know they blame me for your divorce, and before you say it, I know it wasn't my fault *or* their mother's. I understand that, but they don't or won't."

He'd have liked to say it didn't matter, but it did. His one wish was that Adam, Eric, and Jeana would see that he truly loved their father and did everything he could to make him happy.

"That's enough talk about the kids." Jonathon ate another bite before drinking his orange juice and placing the tray on the floor beside the bed. "I have something much more important to talk about."

"And what is that, pray tell?" Greg asked as Jonathon rolled into his lover's thick arms, letting his head rest on Greg's shoulder.

"You, Gregory Mansfield. I'd much rather talk about you," Jonathon flirted as his fingers carded through the salt-and-pepper hair on his lover's chest. "I missed you all week, and I'm glad you're here." Leaning forward, he let his tongue glaze around a nipple, the familiar musky saltiness of his lover's skin bursting onto his tongue. Shifting on the bed, he threw back the covers, and Greg took him into his arms, pressing them together, starting a familiar, passionate dance they'd done together for going on two decades now. Of course, over the years, their flamenco had changed into more of a waltz, but that didn't seem to matter. All that really did was the way they felt for each other.

"You're still amazing, you know that?" Jonathon whispered as Greg held him tight, spooned to his back, his lover's breathing already beginning to even out.

"So are you, Boo," Greg responded sleepily as a hand slowly rubbed circles on Jonathon's stomach.

"Are you feeling all right?" Jonathon asked, rolling over in Greg's embrace, stroking a hand over his forehead, petting him lightly while surreptitiously checking for a temperature.

"I'm fine." Greg tightened his grip, winding a leg between Jonathon's. "The flight was just long, and I didn't get much sleep. I'm not as young as I used to be." Greg paused, his eyes opening. "Or as handsome."

"Stop it." Jonathon smiled. "You're just as handsome at sixty-two as you were the day I met you, and don't you dare think otherwise for a second." Jonathon saw Greg's eyes close, and he slowly got out of bed, dressing quietly before leaving the room to let Greg sleep for a few hours.

Wandering through the house, he stopped dead in his tracks in the kitchen—or what had once passed as the kitchen. It looked as though a bomb had gone off. How anyone could dirty every pan in the house as well as every inch of the granite countertops making eggs, toast, berries, and juice was beyond him, but somehow Greg had managed. Checking out the sink, he picked up a saucepan with congealed oatmeal in the bottom and began to laugh. The man was a wizard in the courtroom, arguments a model of logic and order, and he could write a contract so ironclad an atomic bomb couldn't break it, but in the kitchen, the man could make a chaotic mess faster than a two-year-old on a sugar high. But none of that mattered as Jonathon opened the dishwasher and began placing the pans in their racks after scraping out the remains.

Closing the dishwasher door, he reached for the phone just as it began ringing. Snatching it from the cradle, he answered it fast so it wouldn't wake Greg. "Hello."

"Is Greg there?" He recognized Doreen's voice instantly, wishing he'd checked the caller ID and sent it right to the answering machine.

"He is home, but he flew all night, so he's resting," Jonathon said evenly to the Wicked Witch of Westchester. How Greg had ever seen enough in her to marry her was completely beyond him. Jonathon wanted desperately to tell her to jump on her broom and fly back to Oz, but it would only make trouble for Greg, so he held his tongue.

"Well," her affected accent rang through the line, "I need to speak to him right away." Jonathon knew what that tone and urgency meant.

"You can't," Jonathon said flatly. "He's asleep, and I won't wake him except in an emergency, and your needing money isn't an emergency." He heard her sputter, and he knew he'd hit the nail on the head. "I'll tell him you called and why." Pressing the disconnect button, Jonathon turned off the ringer—it would be just like her to keep calling—and placed the phone back in the charger. Wandering into the living room, he pulled open the patio doors and stepped out onto the deck, looking out over the ocean, listening to the waves crash on the rocks below.

"Who was that?" Greg asked from behind him, and Jonathon turned to see Greg rubbing his eyes like a little boy just waking from a nap, a pair of boxers hanging from his hips. Walking back inside, leaving the doors open to let in the breeze, Jonathon poured Greg a cup of coffee and handed it to him.

"Doreen. She wanted money."

Greg took the cup but just set it on the counter. "Oh." Greg moved closer.

"You need to sleep," Jonathon chided gently as he took Greg's hand, leading him back to the bedroom.

"Can't sleep without you," Greg pouted playfully, and Jonathon climbed back into bed after him, hugging Greg close as he listened to his lover's soft breathing. An hour or so later, Jonathon closed his book, placing it on the bedside table, Greg's arm still resting over his stomach.

"We should get up if we're going to have lunch in the city," Jonathon said softly, kissing Greg's temple, feeling the other man stir, brown eyes fluttering open. "Are you feeling better?"

Greg's answer was to pull Jonathon into a kiss before running his fingers over sensitive ribs. Jonathan giggled and squirmed, trying to get away while at the same time enjoying the touch. "Greg," he cried out through giggles as he tried to tickle his lover back. "We have to get dressed," he managed to say through fits of laughter. "And this family lunch was *your* idea." As much as he disliked the thought of having lunch with Greg's kids, he'd do it without complaint. Greg did plenty for him and asked for very little.

The fingers stopped, leaving both men lying on their backs, trying to catch their breath. Getting out of bed, Greg walked into the bathroom while Jonathon made the bed and carried the dishes into the kitchen, putting everything away before starting the dishwasher and returning to the bathroom. Cracking the door, he heard Greg's off-key singing and smiled. Entering the room, he shaved before pushing back the curtain and joining his lover under the spray.

An hour later, dressed, packed, and ready, the two men left the house, with Greg locking the door as Jonathon carried the last of their bags. "Would you like me to drive?" Jonathon asked, and Greg nodded but motioned toward his blue Mercedes. "You mean we're taking your new baby?" He hadn't paid attention to which car Greg had loaded.

"Well, I was thinking that your car is getting old, and if you like it, we'll get you one." Greg grinned before opening the passenger door.

Jonathon walked around to the driver's side, opening the door and sliding into the seat, soft, saddle-colored leather surrounding him. "Greg, didn't your car have black seats?"

Greg grinned and handed him a set of keys. "Happy Birthday, Boo."

Jonathon sat stunned for a second before hugging Greg tightly. "Thank you. I...."

"It was the only way I could think of that you'd let me get it for you," Greg chided lightly.

"You know how I feel about paying my own way," Jonathon replied, and he started the engine before pulling out of the driveway and onto the street.

"I've told you before, it's not mine or yours, but ours, and I've meant it."

Jonathon turned out onto the main road, en route to the expressway. "I know you do." Even after all these years, he couldn't think of Greg's money as his as well. "And you know how I feel."

Jonathon felt Greg's hand on his leg, squeezing lightly. "That's one of the reasons I love you so much. I never had to worry if you loved me or my money, because you almost never let me spend any of it on you."

Jonathon glanced over and saw Greg relax back in the seat as they entered the expressway, heading into the city. The drive took over an hour, and as they got closer, the traffic got worse. Jonathon normally hated driving in the city, but with Greg tired, he was glad to do it. Pulling up to the restaurant, he handed the keys to the valet, and together they walked into the fine restaurant.

Jonathon immediately saw Greg's children, already seated, and as they approached, he heard their conversation cut out. One by one, they stood and hugged their father and said hello to him, with only Jeana hugging him as well as she wished him a happy birthday. Of Greg's children, she was the spark of life. It had always surprised him that, as the youngest, she was the one who paid the least attention to their mother's rantings about him. "Thank you for inviting us, Dad," she said as she pulled up her chair, reaching for a menu, excitement filling her voice. "Are you doing anything special for your birthday?" she asked, looking to Jonathon.

"We're going to the lake for a few days," Jonathon answered, his own excitement coming through regardless of the boys' stony expressions.

"Lake George? I always love going there in the summer. This is the perfect time to be there."

"No," her father corrected lightly, "we're going to Raquette Lake for a few days."

"Must be nice," Adam grumbled, glowering at Jonathon.

"That's enough," Greg interrupted. "All three of you spent your summers at camp on Raquette Lake, and none of you were deprived of anything. As I told you on the phone, you're all adults, and I expect you to start acting like it."

Jonathon saw Eric's expression soften into shame, and even Adam looked contrite, at least for a few minutes.

"So, Dad, did you actually get to meet Harry Jenkins, All-American?" Adam sounded almost skeptical, but he continued. "Is he as cool in person as he is in on television?"

Jonathon could see the conflict on Greg's face, knowing he wanted to make his son happy but couldn't say much about the man without breaking any confidences.

"He was pretty nice."

Jonathon knew Greg wasn't telling the truth, but it was what his kids wanted to hear. No one wanted to know that someone you admired was the biggest pain in the ass on earth in real life.

The server arrived and they placed their orders; then the conversation turned to school and the classes each of the kids would be taking in the fall. All through lunch, Jonathon kept watching the boys, wondering when something was going to happen, waiting for some barb to be thrown his way, but nothing came. After they'd eaten, Greg excused himself.

"So Jonathon, how's the mining coming?" Adam asked, and Eric snickered into his water.

"Excuse me?" Jonathon put down his fork, telling himself it had been too good to be true.

"Well, since Dad's getting older, we figured you must be digging for gold in the back yard. After all, you're not getting any younger either," Adam commented before adding, "Your looks are definitely fading, so you better get what you can, fast."

Jonathon didn't know how to react, but he could figure out where this idea had come from. "I've never wanted anything from your father except his love," he answered truthfully.

"Yeah, right," Eric scoffed as he slouched in his chair, his lack of backbone becoming a physical as well as emotional characteristic.

"That's enough, you two," Jeana interrupted. "Neither of you have the brains to think for yourselves, so you let Mom do all your thinking for you. You're both pathetic." She shook her head. "Jonathon and Dad have been together for seventeen years. We were just babies when Mom and Dad divorced, and you keep carrying on as though it were yesterday. And why? Because Mom's a mental case."

Thankfully, Greg returned, and the meal ended without further incident. After saying good-bye to their father and ignoring Jonathon, the boys hurried off. Jeana stayed behind for a few minutes while Greg paid the check, giving them each a hug before saying her own good-byes and wishing Jonathon a happy birthday.

"Well, that wasn't bad, was it?" Greg asked as he placed his napkin on the table before standing up.

Jonathon pushed back his chair. "Only if you don't consider that, while you were gone, my profession changed from school teacher to miner, or more specifically, gold digger." Jonathon stood up, throwing his napkin on the chair. He looked to Greg, his face white, body literally shaking.

"The little shits. I'll kill all three of them." Greg glared at the door his children had passed through a few minutes earlier.

Jonathon touched Greg's arm. "It wasn't Jeana, and don't let it upset you."

"You're way too forgiving." Greg's body relaxed, and the glare died out of his eyes. "I suppose I should learn that, as much as I'd like to, I can't undo years of Doreen's poison."

"I wish you could." Jonathan walked toward the door with Greg following after him. "Let's put it behind us." Already he could envision the view from the lake house, the loons and ducks calling from the water. "They aren't going to change, and I won't let them spoil the occasion." Stepping outside, he handed the card to the valet, and his car was brought around.

It took a while to get through the tunnels and out of the city, but soon the dense population gave way to suburbs, and then woods and fields. "I love the car," he told Greg. "It drives like a dream." His answer was a soft snore, and Jonathon smiled as he continued driving. Around Albany and then further north into the Adirondacks, Greg remained asleep as they continued north, past lakes and through forested roads where the trees grew together overhead.

"Where are we?" Greg stirred, stretching within the confines of the car.

"Almost there," Jonathon answered as he made the final turn onto Route 8. "We're only about twenty minutes away."

"I slept that long? You should have woken me."

"It's okay. You know I love this drive, and you needed your rest." Jonathon reached across the seat, stroking Greg's leg, and felt his lover's hand take his. They rode in silence—words weren't needed—and Jonathon could feel the muscles in Greg's body relax the closer they got to the lake and the farther they got from civilization. Greg's cell phone chirped softly, and he turned it off; there was no cell phone service at the lake. Making the last turn, Jonathon drove into the small village and parked the car. Getting out, he stood by the door, breathing deeply, letting the scent of the woods and lake fill his senses. "Let's go into the store."

"You just want doughnuts for tomorrow," Greg teased, but he followed right behind.

Pulling open the screen door, they walked into the general store and were instantly transported back in time. The shelves were wooden, probably built in the forties, canned goods standing on them in small pyramids, wooden floors scuffed with the feet of generations of Raquette Lakers. The entire place was steeped in the smell of freshly made doughnuts with cinnamon sugar, as well as cookies and bread. They'd definitely left the city behind, and damn if it didn't feel good.

"Hey, Jonathon, hey, Greg, how long are you staying?" the girl behind the counter asked as she walked to the doughnut case.

"Just through the weekend, Lila," Jonathan answered with a smile. "How's the weather been up here?"

"A little cool. You'll need a sweatshirt or jacket after dark, but otherwise it's been darned nice. You want your usual half dozen?" She inclined her head toward the case.

"You bet, and a few of those cookies your mother makes would be great too." He looked over at Greg, who was picking up sweatshirts. "You need one?"

"Yeah, Boo, I do." He brought one over and placed it on the counter.

"Is there anything else?"

"Not right now, but we'll see you for more goodies." Jonathan paid, and after saying good-bye, they headed out.

At the docks, Jonathan removed the cover from their small boat. When they'd first bought the cabin, they had just had a fishing boat with a motor. After the first time they'd gotten caught in the rain, Greg had bought a larger boat with a Bimini top. After transferring their gear from the car to the boat, Greg parked the car while Jonathon started the boat motor, and soon they were skimming over the surface of the water, Greg at the wheel, Jonathan sitting next to him.

Greg took his time, like he usually did, keeping the speed down and letting the peacefulness of the lake, trees, and sky work their magic. A few homes could be seen, but most of them sat back far enough that most of the lake looked like the trees came right to the water, like they were in the middle of nowhere.

Almost at the far north end of the lake, Greg slowed the motor and eased the boat against the dock. Jumping out, Jonathan secured the craft, and Greg cut the engine. The sound echoed for a split second and then faded away. There was nothing to replace it except the slosh of the water on the shore and the birds calling from the trees.

The sun was already starting to set by the time they'd hauled everything up from the dock to the four-room log cabin. Outside and in, the place was rustic domesticity at its best. Carrying the suitcases inside, Jonathan placed them in their bedroom, the larger of the two. He loved this room, with its log walls, pine plank ceiling, pine windowsills, and rough beams.

"Would you like me to unpack in here while you check out your kitchen?"

"Okay," Jonathan answered, "but I'll meet you on the porch in twenty minutes."

"Deal."

Jonathan checked out what had been provided and smiled when he saw fresh steaks, chicken, and a foil packet marked "use first" in rough script. "Looks like lake trout for supper." God bless their caretaker, Winston, a lifelong laker and their neighbor one cove up.

Grabbing two beers from the fridge, Jonathon carried them to the porch, setting them on a table before standing at the birch-branch railing, looking out over the water. It wasn't long before a pair of arms snaked around his waist and a head rested on his shoulder. "When you asked to buy this place ten years ago, I didn't understand why." Greg's breath tickled his ear.

"Do you know now?" Jonathon leaned into the touch as a loon called to its mate from the lake below.

"The peace and quiet gets into the soul. I didn't know how much I needed it."

"That's why I bought it, but not why this place is so important now." Jonathan turned in Greg's embrace. "This place is important now because when we're here, you're mine and mine alone." Jonathan couldn't help hugging Greg tightly. "There are no phones, no office, no kids, no courts, no lawyers," he whispered in his lover's ear, "and before you say it, you don't count. You're not a lawyer when you're here. You're just my lover. That's why this place is so important. I would have sold everything I owned to have a place like this with you." Jonathon felt a hand on his hair, petting softly. His emotions were very close to the surface, and he didn't look up.

"I love you too, Boo." He heard a slight break in Greg's voice.

After they had stood together for a while, holding each other, Jonathon finally stepped back. "I need to make some dinner. Why don't you relax a while and we'll eat out here? It's a perfect night." He leaned toward Greg, and they shared a kiss before he moved inside.

Jonathon made a simple dinner of pan-seared trout in butter with a light salad. Carrying the plates onto the porch, he found the small table set between their chairs, two candles in the middle. They ate quietly, their eyes traveling from each other to the now-moonlit expanse of water to the canopy of stars that seemed so close they could reach out and touch them. "There's ice cream for dessert, if you want it," Jonathon commented as he carried the plates inside, returning with two more open beers.

"No thanks," Greg answered softly, and then Jonathan found himself pulled across his lover's legs. "There's only one thing I need for dessert, and it certainly isn't ice cream." Greg swigged his beer, holding him tightly, and Jonathon leaned against Greg's warmth as the chill of the night crept around them on its way into the cabin.

When the beers were finished and the candles sputtering, Jonathon blew them out, standing at the railing once again. This time, Greg didn't hug him like he had earlier. Instead, Jonathon felt a tug at the hem of his shirt just before it was lifted and tugged over his head. "Come inside, Boo."

The cool air raised goose bumps on his arms, and Greg held him close as they moved indoors and into the bedroom. Greg pulled back the hand-sewn quilt Jonathon had purchased years before. Hands felt for his belt, opening it before parting his pants and slipping them down his legs. Climbing onto the bed, Jonathon watched as Greg stripped in the moonshine reflecting off the lake and through the open windows. First that barrel chest, strong and full; then the hips and waist, wider than they used to be but still trim; legs, thick and strong. The bed dipped and Greg curled next to him, pulling the blanket up over them both, the lake breeze providing fresh air and coziness.

Greg shifted adeptly and Jonathon found himself on his back, his lover on top of him, eyes shining. "Happy birthday." Greg kissed him, hard and with a deep, abiding passion that Jonathon felt swell in his heart.

"Best birthday I can remember," Jonathon sighed as Greg dipped his head, circling a nipple with his tongue. "And I remember each and every one." He groaned, back arching, mashing his chest to Greg's lips.

Greg held him tight as they kissed like their lives depended upon it, the intensity surprising Jonathon as he let himself get swept up in Greg's wave of passion. They made love regularly, always had, but as the years went by, it had definitely become more sedate, more familiar and expected. Not tonight. "Love my Boo," Greg gasped against his lips as Jonathon cupped his beefy butt, kneading the cheeks, fingers sliding to tease and caress.

Legs parted his, and Jonathon pushed the covers down, locking his ankles around Greg's waist. "Want the best birthday present possible."

"You sure? Don't want you to be sore tomorrow when we're on the lake all day." There was nothing but concern in Greg's voice.

"Yes," Jonathon hissed as a finger breached him, "that's it!" There was no way he was going to turn down a second time today with Greg. As his lover had aged, lovemaking once a day was all they could expect, but with him raring to go, Jonathon was more than ready and willing. "Make me yours again. Show me!"

He felt Greg shift and knew he was reaching to the nightstand. Jonathon closed his eyes, watching Greg in his mind, seeing him as he always did—young and virile. The bed shifted again and Jonathon parted his eyelids, seeing the same young Greg looking back at him. No matter what, those deep, rich eyes never changed, always looking on him just like they had when they first met.

Blunt and full, Greg pressed into him. "I'll be slow, Boo."

"Don't want slow, want you." Jonathon pressed forward, taking Greg's thickness in a rush that drove the breath from his lungs, filling him with love. "That's it," Jonathon cooed softly, muscles squeezing, that familiar burn fading quickly. Greg slid out, pressing back inside, slowly at first, but picking up speed. "Just want you," Jonathon murmured as he stroked his hands over his lover's warm skin.

"Want you too," Greg cried softly as he thrust deep, joining them together body and soul.

Accompanied by a Waltz

Jonathon stroked himself in time to Greg's thrusts, watching every movement of his lover's body in the reflected moonlight, hair mussed, mouth open, eyes shining. He knew every inch of that body as though it were his own—from the appendix scar on his side, to the way his butt indented on the sides, to the little mark on his chin that no one but he ever noticed—and every inch of it was stunningly beautiful. "So close," Jonathon cried, knowing from his breathing that Greg was right there as well. Stroking a few more times, Jonathon felt the fullness inside him thicken as they went over the precipice together, adding their cries to the sounds of the lake.

Jonathon felt Greg's hands on his cheeks, caressing softly as they remained joined together. Greg kissed him gently, softly, communicating the love they both felt for each other even as Jonathon gasped and shivered when Greg slipped from his body. Getting up, Jonathon got a cloth from the small bathroom, cleaning them both up before rejoining Greg in the bed. The cool night left the room chilly, and Greg's warmth felt heavenly. Curling next to him, Jonathon could already hear Greg's even breathing as he, too, succumbed to the natural calm of this place.

When he awoke to the sound of water birds and small animals skittering through dry leaves, Jonathon felt like he could tackle the world. Stepping onto the cool, wood floors, he did a familiar dance as he rushed to the bathroom. By the time he returned, Greg was stirring. "The lake awaits," Jonathon whispered in Greg's ear, and his lover came instantly awake. A quick dressing and an even faster breakfast later, they saw the sun peeking over the trees, ringing the water as they walked to the boat, Greg carrying the fishing equipment, Jonathon carrying the food. Stowing the gear, Greg turned the key, and the motor roared to life. They were off, traveling to Greg's "secret" fishing spot. Camps and cabins passed as they trolled inlets and coves—camps that had once belonged to notables with last names like Huntington and Carnegie, cabins that ranged from rustic to palatial, but none of it mattered to Jonathon, because all he could see was his Greg.

They spent their days fishing, catching nothing, but that didn't matter—nothing did other than their time together. At night, they made love, sleeping curled together, and let the world slip away, if only for a while.

Their last afternoon, Jonathon took the boat over to Winston's to thank him for his help and make arrangements for the next six months. Summer was fading fast, and he wasn't sure they'd make it up again, although he hoped they'd get a chance in the fall. As he was motoring back, the sky darkened and the wind came up, blowing in his face hard and fast. As he pulled up to the dock, the first drops hit the windscreen. Snapping on the cover, Jonathon hurried to the cabin, getting soaked to the skin as the sky opened up.

"Go take a shower," Greg suggested with a smile on his face. "I'll make some cocoa and we can sit and listen."

Showered and warm in sweatpants and a thick sweatshirt, Jonathon stepped through the house to the porch, where he found Greg asleep in a chair, a book on his lap, glasses askew, cocoa in mugs on the table, completely forgotten. Finding a blanket, he draped it over him, kissing the wrinkled forehead just below the graying hair before walking back inside, curling on the sofa with a book.

Dinner they made together, eating on the porch as the rain soaked the earth and water dripped from the eaves in a soothing serenade of nature's music. "Tonight's our last night," Greg said softly as he sipped the last of his wine. "Tomorrow we go back."

Jonathon noticed that Greg didn't say "home." "I love it here, and I love how you are when you're here."

Greg nodded his head, resting it against the back of the chair. "I always feel recharged."

Jonathon set down his glass. "Are you willing to spend some of that stored-up energy?" He winked playfully as he knelt on the rug, resting his head in Greg's lap.

"I'm willing to let you spend some of your energy." Greg tilted his head, and Jonathon met his eyes. "Let's go inside." Greg took his hand and Jonathon followed, letting his lover lead them to the bedroom. "Make love to me, Boo," Greg said softly.

Accompanied by a Waltz

Jonathon nodded slowly before stripping them of their clothes. Their lovemaking was slow and tender, accompanied by soft gasps, sweet nips, and silent cries, with the gentle rain and the drip from the roof keeping time.

In the morning, clouds seemed to reach almost to the water as Jonathon finished his coffee on the porch, listening to Greg as he moved around the cabin, packing the last of his things. Taking the last sip, he sighed softly before walking inside. While he was standing at the sink, washing the mug, a warm body pressed to his back.

"I know you hate to leave; I do too. We'll come back for the Columbus Day holiday weekend."

Somehow, deep down, he believed Greg but knew it wouldn't happen, for whatever reason. The conflicting feelings made him shiver.

"You getting cold?" Greg asked, holding him closer.

"No, I'm fine, just a little sad," Jonathon replied, turning around, stealing a kiss, which turned into two. "We'd better get going or we'll get home too late."

Greg released him, and Jonathon hauled their bags and trash to the boat while Greg closed up everything before following down to the dock and climbing into the boat. The clouds and gray water echoed Jonathon's feelings as they moved across the water. No taking their time and enjoying the ride this time—Jonathon opened the engine full-throttle, skimming over the lake, slowing only when they entered the channel, slipping into their spot at the dock. After tying up, Jonathon unloaded their things while Greg brought around the car. Waving to friends, they loaded and said brief good-byes before starting the trip home.

Jonathon drove, and he noticed Greg fidgeting in his seat before dozing much of the trip. "You okay?" Jonathon asked softly and got a squeeze on the leg and a smile as a response.

"Just a little indigestion." He burped loudly to accentuate his point, and Jonathon rolled his eyes.

"Proof wasn't necessary, dear."

They both laughed and then settled into a quiet conversation for the last hour. Pulling into their drive, Jonathon hit the opener and pulled into the garage. "Go on, open the house. I'll bring in the bags," Greg said as he opened his door.

"Okay." Grabbing the cooler from the back seat, Jonathon unlocked the door, dropping the cooler on the counter before opening the patio doors and sliding open windows to let the sea breeze air out the house. After unpacking the cooler into the refrigerator, he put it in the closet before wandering back outside to see what, or more likely who, was keeping Greg.

Walking between the cars in the garage, he saw the open trunk and wandered to the back of the car. He found Greg slumped over the back of the car, his head and torso resting on the suitcases in the trunk. "Greg!" Jonathon shook a shoulder but got no response. Lowering him to the pavement, he realized he wasn't breathing and began CPR.

"Mr. Pfister, is he okay?"

Jonathon glanced up for a second and saw Joshua, the seven-year-old from next door, standing wide-eyed on the lawn that separated their driveways. "Have your mom dial 9-1-1." Tears streamed down his face as he continued chest compressions, followed by mouth-to-mouth. "You can't die, you just can't die," he chanted under his breath. Other people rushed over, and Herbert, an orthopedic surgeon from across the street, took charge, relieving him, while his wife, Sheila, took over the breathing. Stumbling back, Jonathon leaned against the car, hand over his mouth, repeating for Greg not to leave him as sirens howled in the distance, becoming louder and louder.

Paramedics arrived and Jonathon backed away farther, getting out of the way, but not so far that he couldn't see his love. Herbert began barking orders almost before the truck stopped. Needles appeared, and Greg's shirt was cut open. Herbert raised a huge needle, and Jonathon turned away, unable to watch. He felt almost invisible until one of the neighbor ladies stood next to him, taking his hand in her wrinkled one, talking to him softly. He couldn't hear what she said, but her tone told him she understood.

Someone yelled, "Clear!" and he saw Greg's body jump and flop on the ground. Herbert listened and then shook his head. Jonathon walked to Greg, pushing by the paramedics and around the equipment and supplies scattered on the ground. Dropping to his knees, he clenched his eyes closed, willing Greg to wake up and the scene to change. Opening his eyes, it looked the same. Greg was still on the ground, unmoving, and Jonathon knew his love would never move again. Lifting Greg's hand from the concrete, Jonathon held it to his cheek, weeping softly until someone led him away.

CHAPTER Two

Ten months later

STARING at the bronze urn as though it were the Holy Grail, Jonathon sat, unmoving, in Greg's chair in the living room of the Raquette Lake cabin, a blanket wrapped around him against the morning chill. At least this time he'd remembered the blanket. Tears welled in his eyes, falling silently down his cheeks, staining the blanket where they dropped. He'd long stopped trying to dry them; it didn't work anyway. The only time he'd been able to keep them at bay was when he'd been at work. His third-graders had been like a balm of life for him when he was teaching, but other than that, he was a mess. He knew it, and he just didn't give a damn. Pulling the blanket tighter, he brought the fabric to his nose, breathing deeply, Greg's scent faint but still there, making the tears fall faster.

In his will, Greg had asked Jonathon to scatter his ashes on the lake, but he hadn't had the heart to do it, so they sat on the mantel where he could look at them. In fact, they were never very far away from him. At home, he kept them in the bedroom on the dresser. Here, he'd placed them on the mantel as soon as he'd arrived a week ago, and he'd barely managed to take his eyes off them.

Hours later, a low rumble reached Jonathon's ears, but he ignored it, still sitting in the chair, lost to the world and to himself as he wallowed in grief that showed no sign of ending. Not that he wanted it to; his grief was all he had left of Greg now—that and the urn. The sound got louder, and Jonathon's brain processed it as a boat motor, dismissing it as he had the others that passed by. But this one got louder still. Standing up, he walked to the screen door, looking out as the boat he didn't recognize pulled up to his dock. Turning away, he closed the thick pine door and retreated back to his chair, having no intention of talking to anyone. He ignored the knock a few minutes later that turned to pounding.

"Go away!" he called to the door, not even vaguely interested in who was behind it.

"Jonathon." He knew that voice. "Open the door."

Getting up, he walked to the door, pulling it open before slamming it shut again. "What part of 'go away' don't you understand?" Without further comment, he walked back to his chair.

The door opened slowly, "Fuck," Jonathon swore. "I knew I should have locked the goddamn thing." He didn't even turn to look. "What do you want, Marty?"

"Jonathon," he answered softly, "you have to come back."

"I don't have to do anything!" he yelled to the walls.

"Yes, you do," Marty replied as he stepped closer. "You need to come back. The hearing is tomorrow, and you have to be there."

"I can't do this," Jonathon whispered as he pulled the blanket higher, hoping it would just make him disappear.

"Jonathon," Marty snapped harshly, making him turn his head, "you have to." A chair scraped across the floor. "I've been Greg's friend for over forty years. Hell, the only reason I made it through law school was because of him. He was the best man I ever knew, and I won't let anyone disparage his memory or his legacy. I loved him almost as much as you do, and there's no way you can let Doreen and those boys try to break his will and go against his wishes. He was very clear about what he wanted, and he spelled it out for you and the rest of the world. You have to do this."

"I don't think I can." Jonathon turned toward Marty and felt the older man hug him tightly. The last of Jonathon's tenuous hold on his emotions broke, and he sobbed against the man's shoulder. "I don't *want* to go on without him."

"You have to, Jonathon," he heard Marty whisper softly in his ear. "Greg wouldn't want you to feel this way. You know that. All he ever wanted was for you to be happy. It would break his heart to see you like this." Marty let go and settled back in his chair.

Jonathon wiped his eyes, hanging his head. "I don't have the strength."

"Yes, you do," Marty corrected forcefully. "Because if you don't, then everything Greg worked for, worked so hard to give you and help provide for you, will ultimately end up under the control of his shrew of an ex-wife." Marty stood up, and Jonathon saw him looking around the room. "God, don't you pick up after yourself?" Marty bent down and began gathering things off the floor. "And when was the last time you shaved?" Marty crinkled his nose. "Or bathed, for that matter?"

Jonathon didn't want to think about it, so he just sat there, hoping all this would go away.

"Up!" Marty tilted the chair forward, practically dumping him on the floor. "I'm not going to allow this, and I'll kick your butt all the way back to Long Island if I have to. So get your ass moving." Marty grabbed the blanket, pulling it off Jonathon's shoulders. "Go get showered and cleaned up. We're leaving in an hour. You can come back and wallow in self-pity after the hearing, but right now, you have someone I care very much about to take care of."

Jonathon found himself walking toward the bedroom, stopping in the doorway. "I know you really loved him too."

"I wasn't talking about Greg." Marty stopped what he was doing, standing still. "I was talking about you."

That stopped Jonathon in his tracks and almost had him hugging the man again, but he didn't have the energy. Closing the door behind him, he stripped off the clothes he'd been wearing for God knew how long, leaving them in a pile on the floor before walking into the bathroom. Standing in front of the mirror, he actually took a step back when he saw himself: eyes puffy and red, face sallow and unshaven, hair uneven and tangled. He looked old—hell, he *felt* old. Rummaging in one of the drawers, he found some shaving cream.

An hour later, showered, shaved, and dressed, Jonathon opened the bedroom door. "Well, look who rejoined the land of the living," Marty commented in a sort of singsongy way. "Does this mean you'll go back with me?"

"Yeah, I'll go back, but once it's over, I'm coming back here." He crossed his arms over his chest. "It's quiet, and I can think."

"More like wallow." Marty threw up his hands when Jonathon started to turn around again. "Okay, okay, if that's what you want to do, I won't stop you... not that I could."

"Good." Jonathon lowered his arms. "Let's get things loaded in the boat, and on the way home you can tell me all about this hearing and what it is I need to do."

"Okay."

Now that he'd decided to go and get this settled, he found he had some energy. Getting the things he'd need together, Jonathon carried them to his boat. Sending Marty ahead, Jonathon looked around the cabin and then walked to the mantel, kissing his fingers and touching the outside of the warm bronze urn before turning and leaving the cabin.

"TOMORROW is just a hearing, not a trial," Marty explained as he drove down the expressway. "I don't think the judge is convinced that the suit Greg's sons are bringing has much merit, and he doesn't want to waste court time on something frivolous."

Jonathon tried to relax but found it impossible. Now that he'd left the quiet of the cabin, he felt strangely disconnected from everything around him. "So what do I need to do?"

"Just be yourself," Marty began. "As your lawyer and Greg's best friend, I intend to show that Greg knew exactly what he was doing when he drew up his will and that his kids and you are bound by its terms. Their lawyer, quite frankly, is going to try to depict Greg as unbalanced and under someone else's influence."

"Mainly me." Jonathon hated the sound of that. They were going to try to paint him as a gold digger. "Wonderful."

"Actually, it's not all that bad, because you haven't behaved that way, and there are plenty of people who're taking your side. But Greg *did* buy you a very expensive car, as well as the cabin, which alone is worth a small fortune."

Jonathon struggled against the seatbelt, looking around. The car suddenly seemed so small and confining. "I loved him, and I never asked for the car. When we bought the cabin, it was Greg who insisted it be in my name."

"I know that," Marty said smoothly, "and I've never doubted it for a second. I'm not saying I think it's true. I'm just telling you what the other side is going to be trying to prove."

Jonathon felt like sinking through the floorboards of the car. "How do I stop them from reducing a seventeen-year-long, loving relationship to what sounds like a cheap, tawdry affair? He was the one person who loved me for me. In my entire life, he was the only one who loved me and didn't expect anything in exchange, except a return of that love." Jonathon stiffened, turning in the plush seat. "If they want everything, I'd give it to them if I could have Greg back. Every cent is meaningless without him." Jonathon felt the tears threaten again.

"That's how you prove it, by being honest and genuine. You know as well as I that this whole thing is because of Doreen. If nothing else, she's hoping to get control of her children's trust funds. And by the time those kids reach twenty-five, there won't be a cent left, because she'll have spent it all and those boys will have allowed it."

Marty clenched the steering wheel. "Don't you see that even though you're opposing them, you're also doing what's best for them? They may not see it now, or ever for that matter, but you're giving them a chance their own mother wouldn't. Greg knew that—why do you think he made you trustee? Because he trusted you more than anyone else in the world, and he knew he could rely on you. That's love in my book." Marty's attention turned back to the road as they made their way around the city.

Darkness fell as they approached the house he and Greg had shared for much of their life together. "Thank you, Marty." He turned to look at the man. "For everything."

Marty turned into the driveway, stopping the car and shutting off the engine. "When Greg first told me he was divorcing Doreen to be with another man, I thought he was throwing his life and career away, but after seeing the two of you together all these years, I realize that he wasn't throwing anything away. The day he chose you was the day he truly started to live." Marty unhooked the seatbelt, drawing Jonathon into a hug. "Ruthie would kill me if I didn't offer you a home-cooked meal and our guest room for the night."

Jonathon found the ghost of a smile trying to form. "You tell Ruthie that I'll take her up on that meal real soon. I was serious about going back to the cabin, but maybe you and Ruthie could come up for a weekend this summer." He almost said that Greg thought it the best place on earth to think, but he couldn't say the words as a huge lump formed in his throat. Jonathan had no idea how he was going to talk about Greg in front of strangers tomorrow, but he'd find the strength to do what Greg wanted.

"I don't know if I can get Ruthie away from Wegman's or Bloomingdale's for more than three days," Marty chuckled. "All kidding aside, I think that would be great." Marty helped him get his things out of the car before pulling away, rolling down his window. "I'll be by at eight to pick you up." The window rose and, with a wave, Marty was gone.

Sighing deeply, Jonathon picked up the bags and walked down the now-scruffy walk, with shrubs and plants that he'd once tended by hand now overgrown and rambling. Ignoring them because he just didn't have the energy, Jonathon unlocked the door and went inside the empty house. Carrying his bags to the laundry, he unloaded their contents into the washer and started it. Leaving the suitcases in the laundry room, he found himself wandering the house. Stopping in the living room, he picked up one of the pictures on the mantel, running his finger over Greg's smiling face. "I'm sorry I'm such a mess," Jonathon whispered, staring down at the picture.

The buzz of the washer pulled him out of his daze. Without thinking, he transferred the clothes to the dryer and put in another load. Opening the empty refrigerator, he shook his head and closed the door once again. He knew part of the problem was that he didn't have anything to do. The house was empty, the cabin was empty, and his life was empty.

Opening the patio doors, he stepped outside, listening to the sound of the ocean until the machines buzzed again. Finished with the laundry, he wandered into the bedroom, stripped and remade the bed, throwing the sheets in the washer before cleaning up and climbing under the covers.

This was the hardest part, and it had been for the last ten months. Most days he could function just fine, but the nights.... Jonathon turned onto his side, trying to calm his mind, but it just wouldn't stop. Images of Greg with him in this bed, the touch of his hand.... "Stop," he said to his own mind. Rolling over again, he curled his arms around Greg's pillow, hugging it, willing his mind to stop whirring as he closed his eyes.

"Jonathon!"

He started awake, hearing footsteps.

"Jonathon, are you up?" Marty's voice rang through the house.

"Give me a minute, Marty," he called as he blinked and looked around the sun-drenched room. Before he could get up, the bedroom door opened and Marty raced inside.

"Good God, Jonathon. We have to be in court in less than an hour. You have five minutes to get ready or we'll be late."

"Okay, Marty, just give me a minute." Jonathon pushed back the covers, feeling better than he had in months. "I dreamed of Greg last night."

"What does…?"

Jonathon held up his hand. "He told me he loved me. I've dreamed of him for months, but I always woke before he could say that. Last night he did." Jonathon hurried toward the bathroom to get ready. If he was going to do battle for what Greg wanted, then he was going to look his best doing it.

JONATHON climbed the steps slowly, feeling dwarfed by the mammoth columns and no more than a face in the crowd as a steady stream of people filed into the neoclassical building, waiting to go through metal detectors and security. With Marty right behind him, fussing like a mother—he swore the man spit-rubbed his cowlick—Jonathon walked through the security section and into the courthouse.

"We're on the second floor, room 205."

"What am I supposed to do again?" Jonathon asked, getting nervous and a little excited at the energy and tension that buzzed around him.

"Shhh," Marty responded, guiding them toward the elevator.

Jonathon got the message: no questions out here in the hallways where someone might interfere. Why, he had no idea. It wasn't as though their case was something of national security, but he followed Marty's guidance and used the opportunity to look around the imposingly massive building with its dark woodwork. Huge chandeliers hung from the ceiling, looking almost as though they were forged at the birth of the city, which of course was the illusion being projected. The elevator doors opened and humanity surged forward, filling the cars for the ride up.

In the hallway outside the closed doors of the courtroom, Jonathon saw Adam and Eric, with Doreen standing nearby, in what looked like a heated discussion with Jeana. The two boys turned away when they saw him coming. But Jeana smiled at him as she wrenched her arm away from her mother and walked over to him and Marty, throwing her arms around Jonathon's neck. He and Jeana had always gotten along, but her display of affection still took him by surprise. "They're such mama's boys, they won't fart unless she says it's okay," Jeana said as she glared at her mother.

"Should we be talking?" Jonathon asked, turning to Marty.

"Jeana's not a party to the lawsuit."

The young woman scoffed loudly. "Of course I'm not. This whole thing is stupid." Her comment gave Jonathon a boost of confidence that he could really do this.

"What was that about with your mother?"

Jeana's face brightened into a wicked smile. "She's just upset because I told her yesterday that I was a lesbian"—Jeana raised her voice—"and she can't handle it." She made sure her mother heard the last part. "I can't take any more of that woman," she added as she shot daggers at her mother. "After this is over, I have something I'd like to ask you."

The doors to the courtroom opened, and further discussion died away as Jonathon followed Marty down the aisle and to a table at the front of the room. Marty set down his case and motioned Jonathon to his chair. Jeana sat in the gallery behind them. The lawyer for the boys took the table across the aisle with Adam and Eric.

The judge entered, and everyone stood. She took her place at the bench and motioned for them to sit. "I want to stress to all parties that this is not a trial, but a preliminary hearing to determine if this case should proceed."

Jonathon felt himself shaking in the chair, his leg and foot bouncing. Marty leaned over to him, whispering, "There's nothing to be nervous about. Just relax and you'll do fine." A soft, warm hand touched him on the shoulder, and Jonathon turned around, Jeana giving him a reassuring smile.

"Mr. Pfister, are you prepared?" She directed her gavel to their table.

"He is, Your Honor," Marty answered, and Jonathon found himself nodding slightly.

"Very good." She turned her attention to the other table. "Mr. Weatherby, I will only give you so much latitude here. This family has suffered a loss, so make any points you want, but do it quickly and with sensitivity."

"Yes, Your Honor."

"Good. I've read your briefs, and it's your intention to prove that Mr. Pfister unduly influenced Mr. Mansfield when he made his will." The bailiff stepped forward and administered the oath to all of them, and then Jonathon stepped forward, sitting in the witness box. The interrogation began smoothly enough, with seemingly innocent questions. Then the boys' lawyer began asking Jonathon about his relationship with Adam and Eric's father. He then read off a litany of gifts that Jonathon had supposedly received from Greg, including every birthday and Christmas present. The last items on the list were the Mercedes and the Raquette Lake cabin. "Not bad payment."

Jonathon opened his mouth to respond, but the judge did it for him. "There's no jury to play to, Mr. Weatherby, and I will not tolerate another outburst like that. Do I make myself clear?"

"Yes, Your Honor, I apologize."

"Then continue."

Jonathon was asked about every disagreement, every fight he and Greg had had, with each and every one blown up to monster proportions. Jonathon clarified what he could. "We didn't always agree, but that didn't mean I didn't love him." Mr. Weatherby continued on, and after two hours, Jonathon felt himself tire.

"Your Honor, I'd like to request a recess," Marty said, and Jonathon smiled at the man. He felt wrung out and could barely keep his eyes off his feet. At the cabin, he'd at least felt as though Greg was with him, but here, it seemed as though they were trying to take him away.

"We'll break for fifteen minutes. Counselors, I'd like to speak with both of you."

Jonathon walked down the aisle and out the back doors, seeing no one. In the hall, he got a drink and sat on one of the chairs. Jeana sat next to him, but they didn't talk. *I need you, Greg. More than anything, I need to feel that you're here.* Of course, no answer came, no brilliant revelations from heaven, so he tried to calm his nerves until they were called back inside.

Jonathon walked back to the stand.

"Mr. Weatherby, do you have further questions?"

"No, Your Honor."

"Mr. Silver." She motioned to Marty, and he stood up, walking to Jonathon.

"How long were you and Greg together?" Marty asked in a warm tone, instantly putting him at ease.

"Seventeen of the best years of my life. Greg was everything to me," Jonathon answered, feeling what he was saying.

"What is it you do for a living?"

"I teach third grade at Lincoln Elementary." Jonathon finally started to relax. Marty wasn't going to steer him wrong; he just had to go with him. "I have for the last nineteen years."

"So, you worked all during the time of your relationship with Greg?"

"Yes. Why wouldn't I? Greg had his work, and I had mine. Greg always said I was teaching the lawyers and doctors of tomorrow. He was proud of what I did. Every February, he came into my class dressed as Abraham Lincoln, reciting the Gettysburg address and answering questions about the life of Abraham Lincoln. The kids all loved him." Jonathon could feel Greg's love around him as he remembered the smile on Greg's face and the laughter of the children.

"Did you pay for things?"

"Of course." Jonathon could feel the tightness in his chest ease a little. "I paid for the upkeep and taxes on the cabin." Jonathon turned his head slightly, speaking to the boys. "Greg bought the cabin on Raquette Lake years ago and put it in my name, but I paid the taxes and upkeep afterwards, as well as part of the household expenses."

"Did you influence or try to influence Greg when he wrote his will?"

Jonathon felt a chuckle start from deep inside and he could hear Greg's voice in his mind. "Good Lord, no. When Greg decided he wanted to do something, he was stubborn enough to follow through. To put a fine point on this, I hadn't even seen his will until after he died. We'd never discussed it. He tried a few times, but I didn't want to think about Greg dying. The only thing I ever told him was that I trusted him."

"Did you love Greg?"

Jonathon looked at the opposing lawyer, answering with conviction, "More than life itself. I'd have gladly given everything I have to have him back. I know that can't happen, but I intend to make sure that Greg's wishes are carried out."

"Mr. Pfister, there's just one more point I'd like to clarify. In his will, Greg asked you to scatter his ashes in Raquette Lake. Has this been done?" One of the bones of contention with the boys was that they felt their father's ashes should be placed in the family plot, next to where their mother would eventually be buried.

"No." Jonathon saw the boys look to their mother, relief plain on their faces. "I didn't want to do something that couldn't be undone."

"Where are his ashes now?" Marty asked quietly, just loud enough to be heard.

"In the urn on the mantel in the cabin." Jonathon wiped his eyes. "I'll scatter them eventually as he asked, but I'm not ready to give him up yet."

"Thank you, Jonathon, I have no further questions." Marty stepped back and looked at the other attorney, who stood up, but the judge stopped him.

"Unless you have some earth-shattering revelation to make, I think I've heard enough." The attorney sat down slowly as the judge turned to Jonathon. "You can be seated, Mr. Pfister." Jonathon stood up and walked back to the table, sitting next to Marty, as the judge continued. "I see nothing here that leads me to believe that Gregory Mansfield wasn't completely aware of what he was doing, and I see no evidence that Mr. Pfister tried to influence him in any way. Therefore, I am granting the motion to dismiss this case, but I'm doing so with prejudice." Her gaze traveled to the other table. "I'm issuing an order granting Mr. Pfister the power to deduct all attorney and court costs he encountered from the trust funds set aside by Gregory Mansfield for his sons, Eric and Adam Mansfield. It is my feeling that this case should never have been brought, and is bordering on a frivolous use of court resources." She banged her gavel twice, glaring at Adam and Eric before turning her gaze on Doreen, who seemed to wither under her stare. Then she stood up and left the courtroom.

It was over. Jonathon could almost feel the lake calling to him as he stood up, hugging Marty before walking out through the back of the room. Jeana met them there, hugging him as well. "How about lunch?" Marty asked as he pulled out his cell phone. "I'll get us a table."

The courtroom door opened, with Adam and Eric exiting the court, followed by their lawyer and Doreen. "This isn't over," Doreen said dramatically.

"Actually," their lawyer corrected, "it is. The judge basically admonished us for bringing a frivolous case before the court. You won't get anyone to take the case after this or a judge to hear it." Without another word, he walked down the hall, leaving the three of them standing alone, looking bewildered.

Adam approached him slowly, looking extremely contrite. "Would you please bury Dad in the family plot?"

Jonathon thought for a minute. "As I said in court, I intend to comply with his wishes. His ashes will be scattered on the lake, as he requested. However, I promise not to do it without telling you and allowing all three of you to be there if you like." Jonathon looked at all of Greg's children before stepping away, turning to where Marty was talking on the phone.

"Jeana, are you coming home?" Doreen asked snidely, her displeasure with her daughter extremely evident.

"No. I'm going to lunch with Jonathon." She turned her back on Doreen and her brothers, walking to where Marty was just hanging up his phone.

"Jeana's going to join us," Jonathon informed his lawyer and old friend.

"Of course." Marty smiled as he led the way out of the building to where he'd parked the car.

"What is it you wanted to ask me?" Jonathon inquired once they'd left the building.

"Mom and I are not exactly getting along, and I don't think we ever will again. My classes at Columbia start again in the fall, and I was wondering if I could stay with you until I go back."

"Of course. Our home is always open to you." Jonathon swallowed hard when he realized what he'd said. There were times it still slipped his mind, usually only for a second, that Greg was gone. "Tomorrow Marty's going to take me back to the lake, since that's where we left my car." Jonathon heard Marty groan, but he didn't argue. "You're welcome to stay at the house for as long as you like."

"Jonathon, for Pete's sake." Marty stopped at his car but didn't open the door. "Jeana can take you back to Raquette Lake." He looked at Jeana. "Someone needs to babysit him, because if I see him sitting around moping, like he was yesterday, I'm going to slap him." Marty rolled his eyes before unlocking the car.

"I'm leaving first thing in the morning, one way or another," Jonathon warned. What else could he say to counter Marty's argument? He *had* been moping, and he knew he probably would again.

"I'll go back to Mom's and get my things after lunch and meet you at the house." Jeana practically vibrated with excitement.

"Fine." Jonathon got in the car, waiting until all the doors closed. "But you better be prepared to bait your own hooks. Oh, and you get to clean the fish."

Jeana grinned. "As long as you cook, it's a deal." Jonathon found himself smiling, truly smiling, for the first time since Greg's heart attack.

CHAPTER Three

Present day

JONATHON walked into the dining room on a beautiful June Sunday morning, surprised to find the house quiet. At his usual place, he found an envelope with his name on it. Wondering what was going on, he opened the envelope, pulling out the card, and his breath caught. It was a Father's Day card, the first one he'd ever received, and his hand shook a little. Opening it, he read the inside. It was simple and to the point.

> *Dad,*
> *You fill spots in my heart my father left.*
> *Love you,*
> *Jeana*

Sometime over the past year—Jonathon wasn't sure quite when it happened—Jeana had started to call him "Dad," and he hadn't had the heart to stop her, even though he didn't think it was right for him to be taking Greg's place. It took him a while to realize he wasn't taking his place—Jeana's heart had just gotten bigger to encompass him as well.

"Dad, you up yet?" Jeana called as she walked in through the patio doors, covered by a thick robe, feet dripping water onto the mat.

"Yes." Jonathon walked to the door and kissed her on the cheek. "Thank you for the card." His throat suddenly felt dry, and he cleared it so he could talk again. "Did you have a good swim?"

"Yes. The water's still a little cold, but it felt good." Jeana was one active young lady, and Jonathon had no doubt she turned heads. He was sort of surprised that she had yet to bring someone special home, but Jonathon firmly felt that it was her business, and if she wanted to talk about it, he'd listen. "Are you going to the lake this weekend?"

"I was thinking about it," Jonathon answered as Jeana stepped inside. "But I wasn't sure if you wanted to do something before you leave for Europe. I'll have plenty of time to spend at the lake after you're gone."

Jeana had won a prestigious scholarship to study at the Sorbonne in the fall. She and some friends were going to spend a few months traveling the continent before school started. "I was thinking about that…." A loud knock on the door interrupted her. "Go see who that is and I'll get changed."

Jonathon opened the door to see Marty and Ruthie standing on his doorstep. Opening the screen, he welcomed them inside. "We just stopped by to see how you're doing. We haven't heard from you in weeks," Ruthie scolded lightly as she leaned in for a kiss on the cheek. Jonathon looked to Marty, who just rolled his eyes as if to say, "This was all her idea."

"Aunt Ruthie, Uncle Marty, what are you doing here?"

Jonathon whipped his head around at Jeana's innocent tone and knew he was being had. "What have you got up your sleeve, girl?" he quizzed with mock anger. "I know you're up to something, and you've got Ruthie in on it." He was willing for now to give Marty the benefit of the doubt.

Jeana motioned to the living room, and they all sat down. "Dad, you know I'm leaving for Europe soon, and… I thought you should come too."

Jonathon tilted his head, looking at her like she was crazy—because the girl had gone completely nuts. "You want me to tag along with you?"

Jeana laughed. "Oh God, no." She chuckled. "No offense, but you'll cramp my style, Dad." She even rolled her eyes for added effect. "One of the girls I'm going with, Inge—you met her two weeks ago—she has family in Vienna, and they have a small apartment that they rent, and it's available for the next couple of months. So, I thought you could get away."

Jonathon felt his mouth fall open. "You want me to move to Vienna?"

"Think of it as doing part of the grand tour," Ruthie interjected. "Vienna's one of the great cities of the world."

He turned his attention away from Jeana, glaring at Ruthie and Marty. "You knew about this?" Jonathon saw the high-powered attorney sink into his chair. "And you're here because?"

"Moral support," Ruthie answered, completely unfazed.

"I think I'll need it," Jonathon replied, feeling a little ganged-up on.

"Not for you," Ruthie clarified. "For Jeana."

Now if that wasn't the living end. "So in this grand scheme of yours, what is it I'm supposed to do?"

"Dad, you don't have to go. I was just hoping you'd do something this summer except spend most of it at the cabin, wishing Daddy were still there. He's gone, and you need to move on with your life."

"Have you been watching *Under the Tuscan Sun* again? Because I swear I'm going to hunt down and destroy every copy of that movie in existence."

"Dad," she replied in that indulgent tone that he found impossible to argue with. Besides, Jonathon had to admit the earnest concern in her voice was starting to wear him down.

"I don't even know where my passport is." There, that should shut things down.

Jeana reached into her purse, pulling out a small blue book and handing it to him. "I found it last week." She sat back in the chair. "The apartment's really nice, and it's located between the inner and outer ring roads, so it's easy to get around. Inge says it's a quiet neighborhood, not too far from the opera house. It'll be good for you to get away for a while, meet some new people."

"Why Vienna?" Jonathon found his resolve crumbling.

"Well, if you want the honest truth, it's one of the cities you never visited with Daddy." Damn, the girl knew him so well. "You'll at least think about it?"

"Yes," Jonathon found himself sighing, "I'll think about it."

"Good. Here's the number of Inge's family in Vienna. They're expecting you in ten days." She handed him an envelope. "I got you a first-class ticket from Kennedy to Vienna."

"I said I'd think about it," Jonathon protested.

Jeana ignored the protest, standing up before giving him a kiss. "Happy Father's Day." She seemed so incredibly pleased with herself. Now how in the hell could he argue with that? Besides, she was definitely her father's daughter.

IN THE end, Jonathon didn't argue, at least not too much, and that was why he found himself cruising over the Atlantic, sitting alone in the plane's first-class cabin, drinking champagne and eating filet mignon. Nervous excitement buzzed from his head to his toes. The day after Jeana had given him the tickets, she'd brought Inge over to the house, and he'd called her relatives. To Jonathon's surprise, not only did they seem very nice, but they were welcoming, and an hour later he'd hung up feeling almost like he'd made new friends. They'd even asked him to call when he landed at the airport, and Hanna, Inge's aunt, had said she'd have one of her boys pick him up. They'd sent him pictures of the apartment, their building, even themselves. It had almost seemed as though they were opening their family to him. The thought had overwhelmed Jonathon just a bit.

"So you're actually looking forward to going?" Jeana had asked after he hung up the phone.

"Yes, okay," he'd said with a grousing smile. "I'll admit it. It might be good to get away for a while." Sometimes, in the middle of the night, he'd think of Greg and wonder why he'd been left alone. After two years, he still missed Greg every day, but the loneliness was becoming harder and harder to cope with. "And visit some new places," he added without saying why. They both already knew why.

Jeana had smiled and stood up, taking Inge's hand. The two young women left the house, and Jonathon guessed they were heading to the ocean for some quiet time. Jonathon had sighed, realizing he was jealous. Not of them, but of their relationship.

The remains of his dinner being removed bumped Jonathon's attention back to the present, and as the lights dimmed in the cabin, Jonathon reclined his seat flat, lying back and pulling the fluffy blanket over him. "Greg would have loved this," he mouthed to himself. No, he had to stop that. He was going to be away for two whole months, and he couldn't spend the entire time he was away remarking on how much Greg would like this or that. This was his own adventure, and he had to make it alone. Deep down, Jonathon knew Greg would be pleased that he was starting to move on—he just needed someone to tell his heart. Shutting off the small light, he lay in the dim cabin thinking of Greg, Jeana, and the adventure he was about to have, until he dozed off with a smile on his face.

Waking with a start when the drone of the engines changed, he jerked himself upright, wondering where he was for a second. "Would you like some breakfast?" the flight attendant asked with a slight accent that Jonathon found charming.

"Yes, please."

"If you'll stand up for just a minute, I'll get you settled," she said with softness in her voice, and Jonathon stood up. She efficiently stripped off the cushion cover, folded his blanket, and returned the bed to a chair. "Here's your breakfast menu." She handed him what looked like a printed brochure, with his choices. "If there isn't something to your taste, you can also choose one of the options from business class." She handed him the additional menu before picking up the linens and hurrying away. She returned for his selection and brought it a few minutes later. He ate slowly, savoring his eggs benedict with fresh juice and fruit.

As he was finishing, Jonathon heard the engine sounds change again. His dishes were cleared, and the noise in the cabin increased as trays were stowed, carts put back in their slots, and landing announcements made. As he sat quietly, his nervous anticipatory excitement ratcheted up as his ears popped and the plane descended, touching down at Vienna's airport. Deplaning, passport control, baggage claim, and customs were a breeze, but now he stood in a wide hallway, looking around. He'd called as asked, and Hanna had said she was sending her son, but Jonathon had no idea what he looked like or how to find him. Settling near the wall, he continued looking around.

"Herr Pfister," Jonathon heard over the crowd, and he searched for the source of the call. "Herr Pfister!" A young man ran up to him, sounding out of breath before he began talking in rapid-fire German.

"I'm sorry, I don't speak much German," Jonathon said apologetically when the kid took a breath.

"No, it is my fault. Sometimes I forget," he said a little haltingly, like he didn't speak English very often. "I'm Hans, Hanna's son and Inge's cousin." He held out his hand and Jonathon shook it, surprised at the grip from such a small person. "My car is this way." He pointed toward the far exit and picked up Jonathon's suitcase, lugging the heavy bag as though it were nothing. Jonathon picked up his other things and followed behind, barely able to keep up with the younger man.

Outside, Hans led him to a parking area and opened the hatchback of the smallest car Jonathon had ever seen. Wedging his suitcase in the small cargo compartment, they put his other bags on the backseat. Then Jonathon got in the front seat, buckling himself in. With a rush of energy, Hans bounded into the car, starting the engine. As they left the lot, Jonathon insisted on paying for the parking; he actually had to use his teacher face to get Hans to take his money to pay the attendant. On the airport road, the car took off like a shot, with Hans weaving in and out of traffic. If Jonathon had ever wondered, he now knew what it felt like to go eighty miles an hour in a gumball machine.

"Have you visited Vienna?" Hans asked as he darted around a much larger truck.

"No. I've been to Europe before with my partner. I've been to Paris, London, and parts of Spain, but that was a long time ago." Greg had taken him to Europe for his fortieth birthday, and they'd traveled for the better part of three weeks, but he didn't really feel like bringing up those memories. Not with Hans making his life flash before his eyes.

"Maybe once you rest, I take you. Show you Vienna." Hans pulled off the freeway, and they began to enter the city proper, traveling down a boulevard and turning onto a wide street. The one benefit of the city traffic was that Hans drove slower, and Jonathon found himself looking out of the windows to take in everything. "Our house is in the middle of the ring roads."

"What street are we on?" Jonathon twisted to try to see a sign.

"Operngasse," he answered proudly. "We live in a nice area." Jonathon could see his chest puff just a little. "If we continue ahead, we would go by the opera house. Do you like opera?" he added with a hopeful lilt in his voice.

"Yes," Jonathon answered simply, and then thought better of it, since Hans was keeping up most of the conversation. "Greg loved the opera, and we had season tickets to the Metropolitan Opera in New York." He hadn't renewed the subscription after Greg died. He'd thought of taking Jeana a few times but just couldn't bring himself to do it. The memories were just too strong.

"We have wonderful opera here, some of the best in the world," Hans said, pride again in his voice. Jonathon wondered what he should say and breathed a sigh of relief as they turned onto a smaller side street before pulling up to a small overhead rollup door. Hans got out of the car, lifting the overhead door before getting back inside and pulling into a tiny paved area that already held a car. No wonder this one was so small—it just fit behind the other. "This used to be a small yard, but parking cost a lot, so Oma changed it."

Hans opened his door carefully, and Jonathon got out as well, barely able to open the door far enough to get out. Hans opened the hatchback and pulled out his bags. Jonathon had no idea how Hans was going to get his bags out of the backseat, but he did somehow, and then he led him through a small passage toward the back door.

"Mutti, I'm back," Hans called over the sound of voices coming from the next room. A woman a little older than Jonathon walked in, wiping her hands on her apron. "Mr. Pfister, I'm glad you arrived."

"Please call me Jonathon." He extended his hand, and she shook it before almost pulling him into the other room.

"I am Hanna. This is my mother." She pointed to an old woman working at the stove. "This is Herr Pfister."

The old woman stepped away from her cooking, greeting him in German. Jonathon tried his best to sound polite, reading her body language because he couldn't pick out a single thing she was saying.

"My mother doesn't speak much English, but she said she's happy you are with us and asks if you are hungry." The old woman began talking again, motioning to the table. "She said you need to eat, you're too skinny," Hanna clarified with a smile, turning to her son. "Take Jonathon's things to his apartment and then come eat." The young man hurried away with a smile. "He's a good boy," his mother said softly in that tone only a proud mother uses. "He's going to university soon."

She motioned Jonathon to a place, and he sat down, wondering what was going on. He hadn't realized that, in addition to getting an apartment, he was also getting a family, but that was what seemed to be happening.

A plate appeared in front of him, along with a roll, some meats, and what looked like marmalade. Jonathon looked around to see if the others were joining him, but they bustled around the kitchen with Hans's grandmother, looking at him every few seconds until he took a bite. Hans came back in and sat down across from him. A similar plate appeared, and he ate quickly, speaking to his mother and grandmother in German. Jonathon found his fatigue catching up with him, and he let the sounds swirl without trying to comprehend anything. There was no way he could understand anything anyway; his brain was already beginning to shut down.

When he was done eating, Hans jumped up from the table, grabbing a book bag from near the door and saying good-bye to everyone, including him, before rushing out the door for what Jonathon assumed was school.

"I'm almost done here, and then I'll show you where you'll be staying." Hanna had barely stopped moving since he had arrived.

Jonathon nodded and smiled, taking the opportunity to glance around the room. The house was obviously quite old, but very well-kept and meticulously clean. Jonathon had the feeling that the furniture had been in these rooms for generations. "This is my mother's house," Hanna explained from the sink, "and has been in our family for many years."

"It's lovely," Jonathon replied sincerely, lightly rubbing the smooth arm of the wooden chair. The building and everything in it seemed to emanate a sense of permanence that he hadn't felt except when Greg was around.

"Come," Hanna said as she took off her apron. "I'll take you back."

Jonathon followed her back through the kitchen, waving to Oma, who smiled and nodded in return. He found himself back in the cramped courtyard, and Hanna led him around the cars to the back wall of the property. Jonathon started to wonder what he was in for when she used a key to unlock an almost hidden door. Handing him the key, she pushed the door open and turned on the lights.

Jonathon walked into a kitchen with appliances and a counter against one wall and a small table near the window. "This is the kitchen," she said, stating the obvious. "Here's the laundry." She pointed to the far side of the counter. "I will show you how to use it."

"Thank you," he responded gratefully as he looked at the dials with everything in German. It didn't look like anything he'd ever seen before.

She led the way to a circular staircase in the corner and started climbing, so Jonathon followed. "It's three rooms, as I told you on the telephone. The kitchen's on the ground floor, the living room on the first, and the bedroom on the second." Hanna opened windows as she moved through the rooms, curtains blowing in the breeze. Jonathon climbed to the bedroom, seeing his bags on the floor, sun streaming through windows, a double bed against the only wall with a window. Taking a quick look around, he stepped back down the stairs to the main floor.

"Do you like it?" Hanna inquired, waiting for him.

"It's perfect."

"I know it's not what you're used to in America."

Jonathon shook his head, smiling as he continued to look around. "It's absolutely perfect."

Hanna smiled as well. "I'll leave you, then." She walked toward the door, stopping again for a moment. "Oh, I'm aware that my niece and your daughter"—she swallowed—"care very much for each other. I also know there was another man whom you cared greatly about." Jonathon opened his mouth, but she put up her hand to stop him. "I have no problem with love between two people." Jonathon liked the way she phrased it. "But my mother is very traditional."

A dark look passed over her face, and Jonathon wanted to ask what was wrong, but he didn't dare. That would be way too familiar. But it was plain that something had hurt her.

"And she doesn't take change very well. I can tell she likes you, so just be discreet around her." He saw the slightest dip in her shoulders that wasn't there before as Hanna went to leave. "I'll be at work for the rest of the day, but Mother will be home. If you need anything, she can help. Believe me, she understands more than she lets on, so don't be shy around her." Hanna closed the door behind her, and Jonathon found himself staring, wondering what he'd just been made privy to.

Turning around, he let out a little whoop. When he'd traveled with Greg, they always stayed at the best hotels and ate at world-class restaurants, but he'd never experienced anything like this. Instead of traveling abroad, he was living abroad. Rushing back upstairs to the bedroom, he looked around the room again. There wasn't a closet, but an imposing wardrobe stood in one corner. Unpacking his clothes and putting things away settled the last of his nerves. So, after opening the rest of the windows to catch the breeze, he set an alarm and lay down for a few hours.

Jonathon had barely closed his eyes when he heard the alarm buzzing in his ear. Forcing himself to get back up, he stretched and yawned before stepping downstairs to the bathroom off the living area. Going through his morning routine felt familiar and comforting, and after changing clothes, he headed outside to explore the city that would be home for the rest of the summer.

Jonathon spent much of the day wandering. He ate lunch at a small café, drank an afternoon coffee at one of Vienna's legendary coffee houses, got some maps, and even rode the tram the entire way around Vienna's famous Ringstrasse. He'd even found a grocery store, and his last stop was to buy his food for dinner.

In his apartment, he made dinner and was just sitting down when someone knocked on his door. Opening it, he found Hans standing outside, shifting from foot to foot. "Mama asked me to invite you to dinner." He peeked inside and saw Jonathon's plate on the table. "Oh, I didn't mean to disturb you." Hans turned and began walking back toward the main house.

"You aren't, Hans, not really." Having been alone most of the day, he could use a little company. "Why don't you come back after your dinner and you can tell me all about Vienna." Hans smiled and waved emphatically as he hurried home, while Jonathon returned to his simple dinner.

After putting his dishes away, Jonathon went upstairs to the living room, opening the door to the small balcony and stepping out into the early evening air. He had a view of the car-filled courtyard, and he could see over the wall into the street. Looking down around his feet, he realized he could probably fit a small chair out here, and it would be a great place to have his morning coffee. As he watched, he saw Hans bound out the door and weave his way between the cars. "Evening, Hans," he called and waved. "Come on up."

"Would you like me to show you some of Vienna instead of just tell you?" Hans had so much energy.

"Sure, I'll be right down." Jonathon walked back through the apartment, locking the door behind him before meeting Hans at the courtyard door.

"Do you want to ride or walk?" Hans asked, and Jonathon looked at the small car, not relishing another ride.

"Not in the car." Hans pointed to a scooter in the corner.

"Maybe next time," Jonathon said with a smile, and Hans opened the door to the street. Stepping onto the sidewalk, Hans led him down the street. "It may not seem like it, but this way's faster if you want to get to the Ringstrasse."

Jonathon kept looking around and saw a very young man across the street, leaning against a wall, hips forward. As Jonathon watched, he slipped his hand beneath his shirt, lifting it so Jonathon could see his abs. Hans instantly began yelling and ran across the street. At first, Jonathon thought they were going to fight, but the kid ran off, with Hans standing on the sidewalk, yelling after him. "Hans, what was that for?" Jonathon said as he crossed the street.

"He's a Strichjunge," Hans spat, still looking where the young man had run. "How do you say in English, a rent boy?" Jonathon followed Hans's gaze but said nothing, feeling a little stunned. "This is a nice neighborhood, and we do not want their kind here," he added forcefully as he continued down the street. "I am sorry if my anger frightened you," he added as they approached the corner.

Jonathon tried not to dwell on it. "It's all right."

They continued walking, reaching the wide Ringstrasse, continuing around until they came to a subway station. To Jonathon's surprise, Hans led him down the steps, and he bought a fare card. Getting on the train, Jonathon slipped into himself, thinking of the man—more like a kid really—whom Hans had driven off. The blank look, the mechanical motion.... He could easily imagine the almost soulless feeling, knowing you were selling yourself just to survive for another day in a world that didn't want or care about you. Jonathon shivered as the train began to slow.

"This is Stephansplatz," Hans explained, "the very center of the city." Hans began walking toward the exit, and Jonathon followed through the huge underground station and shopping arcade. Climbing back to street level, they emerged near the edge of a huge open area, dominated by a massive cathedral. "That's Stephansdom," Hans pointed. "It's very old and the heart of the city. During the war it was damaged, but now it's been completely fixed," Hans explained. "I really love the pattern of the tiles on the roof."

Jonathon looked up at the massive structure, glued to his place as he marveled at the fact that parts of the building were approaching a thousand years old. "Can we go inside?"

Hans shook his head. "It's open during the day, but at night they close it except for evening masses. We could come back if you like."

Jonathon couldn't help smiling at the use of the plural. It seemed that he'd made a young friend, and it felt nice to be around young people. There were times—like right about now, as he stifled a yawn—that he just felt old. But he was finding that the energy of youth was definitely contagious. "That'd be nice."

People moved and congregated around them, the huge open square buzzing with activity. Many shops were closed, but that didn't dampen the energy and enthusiasm that seemed to crackle in the air. Restaurant patrons laughed as they ate under umbrellas in outdoor seating areas, their laughter and conversations floating all around, adding to the excitement. Tourists hustled into the shops that were open, reemerging to show off their finds to the rest of their group. "This is the main shopping district. All the best shops are here," Hans began explaining, "The Hotel Sacher is just down the street. It's very famous."

"Is that where the Sachertorte comes from? I've been seeing signs everywhere for them."

"Well," Hans grinned, "that's one of the ongoing controversies. The Hotel Sacher claims to have originated the dessert, but so does Café Demel. No one pays attention except the tourists." Hans leaned close, speaking in a stage whisper. "The best Sachertorte in town is at the Konditorei just around the corner from home. It's even better than Oma's, but don't tell her."

"I promise to keep your secret," Jonathon responded with a conspiratorial smile. "Shouldn't we be getting back? It's starting to get late, and don't you have school tomorrow?"

"Today's Friday." He smiled excitedly, and Jonathon stifled another yawn. "Forgive me. You must be really tired after your flight. We will go back home." Hans began walking back toward the subway station. "Down there"—Hans pointed down one of the side areas—"is the plague column." Hans placed his hand over his mouth. "It sounds kind of funny, but it's dedicated to victims of disease four hundred years ago. It's very beautiful." They kept walking, and Hans continued pointing out notable sites until they reached the subway. Riding back, Jonathon continued looking around, surprised at just how bright and clean everything was. Emerging again on the street, much closer to his apartment, they walked down the sidewalk, lit with the warm lights of the houses spilling from the windows and lights near doors. Movement off to his side caught Jonathon's attention, and he saw the young man from earlier peer at them. Jonathon smiled and lifted his hand in a quick wave before following Hans into the courtyard.

Saying good night, Jonathon unlocked his door, entering his apartment before climbing all the way to the bedroom. Voices mixing with car engines and even music filtered through the open windows. After going to the bathroom to clean up, Jonathon got ready for bed, climbing between the bottom sheet and the fluffy summer duvet that seemed to settle around him, cocooning him in comfort.

Jonathon woke hours later, knowing something wasn't right. Forcing his eyes open, he listened carefully but heard only the soft sounds coming from the street. Shaking his head, sure he must have been imaging things, he lay back down, eyes sliding closed before flying open when the sound repeated, followed by what he was sure were footsteps on the stairs. God, there was someone else in the apartment. Jonathon looked around, trying to find some sort of weapon even as the footsteps reached the living room level.

Rung after rung, he heard the footsteps climbing to the bedroom, paralyzing him with fear. Staring at the stairs, he saw a head emerge, followed by a torso. Jumping out of bed, Jonathon yelled at the top of his lungs, throwing himself at the figure, who screamed back and then disappeared down the stairs with a clunk and then a thud.

Walking cautiously to the stairs, he peered down, seeing a figure sitting on the floor, appearing to rub his head. "Who the hell are you, and what are you doing here?" Jonathon demanded in his best scolding teacher voice that brooked no argument.

"I was going to ask you the same thing," a male voice answered with a German accent, and Jonathon saw him trying to get up.

"Stay where you are or I'll beat the shit out of you!" Jonathon yelled, and he saw the man sit back on the floor.

"I don't doubt it, but you didn't answer my question." The man continued rubbing the back of his head.

"Since when do I answer the questions of a burglar? I mean it, don't freaking move!" Jonathon kept his tone forceful. "Tell me who you are and why you're here," Jonathon demanded. "You have two seconds before I call the police."

To his surprise, the man laughed. "You do that, and you can explain to them why you're in my home."

That stopped Jonathon in his tracks. "Your home? This is Hanna and her mother's home, and I'm renting this apartment. Now get out." The guy made no effort to move toward him, so Jonathon relaxed slightly. "I really suggest you leave." Jonathon reached for his phone.

"Wait, I think I can clear up part of this. I'm Fabian, and Hanna Mueller is my mother."

CHAPTER Four

"YOUR mother," Jonathon echoed softly.

"Yes. Hanna is my mother. You know, tall woman, dark hair, gets driven crazy by my grandmother." His voice became harsh when he referred to Oma. Jonathon saw the man hold up his hand, a set of keys dangling. "See? I didn't break in, I had a key."

Jonathon wasn't sure if he should believe him or not. All those years living in New York had made him skeptical as hell, especially of strangers that showed up in the middle of the night. "Tell me something else." He tried to think of something to ask. "What's your brother's name?"

The man smiled. "Hans. He'll be going to university soon." The automatic softness in the man's voice told Jonathon he was telling the truth. At the very least, he cared for Hans.

"Okay, you can sit in the living room, I'm coming down."

"Not so fast. What about you?"

"What about me? Your cousin Inge helped arrange for me to rent the apartment." Jonathon moved away from the stairs, conscious of every movement from below as he pulled on some clothes. Slowly walking down the stairs, he half expected something funny to happen, but he reached the lower floor without incident.

Turning on a light, he nearly gasped at the man sitting in the chair. Swallowing while pulling his eyes back into his head, he questioned, "So, Fabio, what are you doing here, and why don't you know what's going on at home?" His confusion about what was going on was not enough to stop him from gazing over one of the most handsome men he'd ever seen. "Tall, dark, and handsome" was an understatement when it came to this man. Jesus, he could spend a month in those big, wide eyes alone, let alone the full mouth and olive skin that Jonathon couldn't help following until it disappeared beneath the open collar of his shirt.

"It's Fabian, not Fabio," he corrected. "So, Oma rented out my home." Disappointment was clear in Fabian's voice.

"I don't know anything about your family or what's going on, except your cousin arranged for me to the rent the apartment through my stepdaughter Jeana." Jonathon shook his head. "That sounds way too complicated for"—he glanced at the clock—"three in the morning."

"You can say that again." Fabian rubbed the back of his head.

"Did you hurt yourself?"

"No, *you* hurt me, pushing me down the stairs," Fabian's words sounded harsh, but there was a certain amusement in his eye. "I'll be fine," he corrected. "So, how long are you planning to stay in my home?"

"Look." Jonathon felt his temper rise a little. "Let's get one thing straight—for the next two months, this place is *my* home, and we are not the Viennese version of The Odd Couple. I rented this apartment from your family, and I have the contract to prove it."

Fabian sighed loudly in response but said nothing.

"Fine, I'm going up to bed. The door's downstairs, I suggest you use it."

"I cannot go there," Fabian responded, tilting his head toward the main portion of the house. "Oma does not approve of me."

"I can't imagine why," Jonathon retorted sarcastically. "Breaking into people's homes at three in the morning. I must say I don't particularly approve of you either."

"I didn't break in...." Fabian let his voice drop off as a steady stream of frustrated German spilled forth, and from the heated tone, Jonathon definitely knew there was plenty of swearing involved. "Look, I'll stay here on the couch until morning, and then I'll talk to my mother. Unless you'd rather I slept in the backseat of one of the cars."

"You'd have to fold yourself in half to fit in the car Hans used to pick me up." Jonathon felt a smile threaten. "Fine, you can stay on the sofa, but don't even try to come upstairs."

Fabian scoffed. "Please, your virtue is safe," he replied as he rolled his eyes. "You may be kind of cute, but I think I can resist you."

For a second, Jonathon forgot everything but the "kind of cute" remark, and he smiled at the handsome young man who was putting his feet up, trying to make himself comfortable. Shaking his head, Jonathon went back up the stairs, trying to figure out how he could move the armoire near the stairs without making a ton of noise. That wasn't possible, so he climbed into bed, with sleep quickly overtaking his jet-lagged body.

WAKING with a start to light filtering through the curtains, a thump from the floor below reminding him that he had an unexpected guest, Jonathon got out of bed, figuring he had better check to make sure everything was still intact. Pulling on a pair of jeans and a T-shirt, he walked down the stairs, cautiously aware of any movement. Granted, he was probably overreacting, but it paid to be safe.

Exiting the spiral staircase, he saw the bathroom door open, and before he could turn away, Fabian walked into the room, dark, chiseled chest glistening with water droplets. "Don't worry, I'll be gone in a few minutes," Fabian said as he tugged a soccer jersey over his head. With

Fabian's head hidden for a second, Jonathon let his gaze travel lower, following the trail of dark hair until it disappeared into tight pants.

Jonathon didn't know what to say and didn't want to leave things on a sour note, particularly if Fabian was Hanna's son. "Is your head okay?"

"Yes. I am fine," Fabian answered as he gathered his things, slinging his bag over his shoulder. "Thanks for letting me use my own couch." Fabian walked down the stairs, and then Jonathon heard the door open and close.

"Asshole," Jonathon called to the walls as he walked to the bathroom to get cleaned up. Stripping down, Jonathon turned on the water and used the hand-held showerhead to spray himself down. His soapy hands wandered over his skin. Jonathon's thoughts began to wander too, and an image of Fabian naked flashed into his mind, his imagination filling in all the details his eyes hadn't provided. His body reacted, and Jonathon stood stock-still, hand stopped mid-stroke. "I'm sorry, Greg," he whispered to the air before washing himself quickly and rinsing off as though he didn't trust his traitorous imagination.

Stepping out of the tub, he toweled himself off, almost stepping back in to try to wash off the guilt. He knew it was okay, that he should move on, but Greg seemed to be slipping further and further away from him lately. He hoped that meant he was healing, maybe getting ready to move on. He knew that was what Jeana would say. She'd been urging him to move on for months, but actually thinking of another man, even one as hot as the asshole Fabian, still seemed strange. He knew what Greg would tell him—that it was okay for him to move on. Wrapping the towel around his waist, Jonathon climbed the stairs, picking up the picture of Greg he'd placed by the bed. "I don't want to forget you. I always want to remember what you sounded like, how you laughed, what you smelled like, the feel of your hands on my skin. Sometimes I feel like you're slipping away," he told the smiling picture, running his finger over the smile crinkles at the edge of the lips. "I miss you, but you're not coming back, no matter how much I want you to." Putting the picture back, Jonathon got dressed before descending to the kitchen, making coffee, and then climbing up to the living level and stepping out onto his balcony for some fresh air.

Sipping his coffee, he thought of what he wanted to do.

"Jonathon."

Hearing his name, he looked down, seeing Hans weaving between the cars. "My brother came home." Fabian joined Hans in the courtyard, and Jonathon could see Hans's grin from there.

Jonathon motioned them up against his better judgment, and he heard the door open and close. A minute later, Hans bounded up the stairs, Fabian following behind. "This is my brother Fabian," he said excitedly. Jonathon was about to say that they'd already met, but Fabian put out his hand, shaking like they were just being introduced, so Jonathon went along with it. "He used to live here before he went away for a while, but he's back now." Jonathon motioned toward the chairs, and his guests sat down. "Mutti asked me to tell you not to worry about the apartment. Fabian's going to be sharing my room with me until you leave."

"Did she say when breakfast would be ready?" Fabian asked.

"No." Hans jumped up. "I'll go find out." Hans left, feet clanging down the stairs, door banging behind him.

"Thanks for not blowing my cover," Fabian said as soon as Hans was gone.

"I don't understand what's going on. Why do you feel you need to hide?"

Fabian stood up, and Jonathon knew he wasn't going to get his answer. "Thanks for being, how do you say, cool, with my brother."

Jonathon shrugged. "You're welcome. But I don't like lying to him. He's a good kid who for some reason seems to like me." Jonathon followed Fabian down the stairs and to the door. "For the record, I'm sorry we got off on a bad foot last night."

"No." Fabian turned. "It was my fault. You didn't have to let me stay. I should have been more grateful." As he reached for the door,

Fabian flashed him a smile that Jonathon felt to his toes. "Danke," Fabian said as he opened the door, and Jonathon heard Hans return, he and Fabian conversing briefly in German. Jonathon found himself smiling as he went to finish getting ready for the day, wondering what was going on. He knew it was really none of his business, but he was still curious. Besides, maybe he'd get another of those smiles from Fabian. Dumping out his coffee cup, he washed the few dishes, leaving them to dry before leaving the apartment to explore.

"Jonathon!" Turning around, he saw Hans closing the front door, running down the sidewalk to catch up to him. "Would you like me to show you some things?" The open smile on his young face was refreshing, and he had to remind himself that he wasn't in New York and he needn't pull away as he normally would.

"Don't you have friends your own age?" Hans nodded in response, his smile dimming at Jonathon's question. "Wouldn't you rather spend time with them?"

"But you're my friend too," Hans responded, his smile brightening. "And I learn to speak English better."

"Then what would you like to show me?" Jonathon asked as they made their way toward the main street.

"The Karlskirche. Mutti said they take down the…." Hans stopped walking, thinking hard for a word. "*Gerüst*. Like a ladder, but bigger," Hans explained, trying to get his point across.

"Scaffolding?" Jonathon supplied. He'd seen it almost everywhere the day before. It seemed as though every building had some somewhere, either inside or out.

"Yes." Hans smiled, and Jonathon could almost see him storing away the bit of information. "They will take down the scaffolding soon."

"Shouldn't we wait until they do?"

Hans grinned. "No. You will see." Taking Hans's word for it, Jonathon followed, and they rode the subway again, getting off on the far side of town, walking toward the huge, white, domed church. Hans led him to the entrance. There were two prices, and Hans told him to pay the higher one. Buying two tickets, they walked inside and were surrounded by a Baroque masterpiece. Splendor upon splendor was all Jonathon could think of as he walked down the center of the building. Looking up toward the dome, the magnificent view he expected was blocked by a large, modern platform. Hans pointed at it. "We go up there after you see down here."

Jonathon wandered through the majestic building with its gleaming marble pillars and altar that looked as though the sun permanently rose behind it. Old training attempted to kick in, and Jonathon almost slipped into a pew to kneel and pray, but he didn't, as other memories overshadowed that training. Instead, he looked for Hans, finding him a few pews back, crossing himself before kneeling. Jonathon continued looking around and joined Hans when he was finished. "Are you Catholic?" Hans asked. "We could come here for mass tomorrow if you like."

The question took Jonathon a little by surprise, but it probably shouldn't have. "I used to be, but that was a while ago. I haven't been to church in a very long time." And he had no intention of starting again now. Jonathon desperately needed to change the subject; he didn't want to insult Hans's beliefs, and he knew he would if this line of conversation continued. "Let's go see about going up." Hans nodded and smiled excitedly.

Once they had made their way toward the back, they found themselves at an elevator. They handed the operator their tickets, the doors opened, and they got inside for the short ride up. The elevator doors opened, and the view whooshed the air out of Jonathon's lungs. Stepping away, he walked to the center of the platform, turning slowly. Everywhere he looked, on every side, were brightly colored frescoed figures, more than life size, in amazing detail. Walking to the rail, he looked down and then back at the paintings, realizing that he was seeing them as the artist had, up close. "They were to be seen from the floor," Hans explained. "They were never meant to be seen this close, and when the scaffolding is taken down, no one will again."

"They're amazing," Jonathon breathed, reaching for the camera around his neck, and he began snapping picture after picture.

"We can go all the way up." Hans pointed to a staircase in the scaffolding that went all the way up to the top. "You can see the whole city from up there."

"Have you been to the top before?"

Hans nodded vigorously. "Lots of times." He indicated the paintings around them. "I want to be an art fixer."

"Art restorer," Jonathon corrected lightly.

"Yes, an art restorer," Hans said softly, repeating the words. "We go up?"

"Yes, we go up." The staircase shook slightly as they climbed higher and higher into the dome. As the surface area got smaller, the frescoed figures became fewer but larger. Higher and higher they climbed, the floor below looking very far away. As they approached the top, the cupola formed around them, the area becoming smaller, the painting of a dove that decorated the top getting closer and closer as the cupola pillars were revealed to be just plaster and paint instead of marble. The effect from below was striking, but up close, all the artist's tricks were revealed. Peering out the small cupola windows, Jonathon could indeed see much of the city. He recognized St. Stephen's, where he and Hans had been the night before, as well as parts of the Ringstrasse. "Thank you for bringing me here," he said softly to Hans, who beamed back at him before he, too, became entranced with the view.

"There's the opera house," Hans pointed out before looking out the other side. "And way over there is the wheel at the Prater." He sounded so excited.

Jonathon looked out and found himself getting excited along with his young friend, making a note to take him to Vienna's version of an amusement park as a thank-you for showing him around. "Are you ready to go back down?"

"If you are." Hans turned and began descending the stairs, with Jonathon following behind. Once they reached the platform, they walked to the elevator, waiting their turn to be taken back to the ground floor. "Are you getting hungry?" He already knew the answer, as he suspected Hans was one of those boys who could always eat. The nod and smile only confirmed his thoughts. "Then let's go get some lunch. Where do you suggest? Preferably a place we can eat outside." The elevator arrived and they filed inside, riding down to the main level.

Hans led the way toward the exit. "Do you want to walk or ride the subway?"

Jonathon automatically looked toward the sky, which was blue as anything, the refreshing breeze caressing his skin, and thought, *Perfect.* "Let's walk." Jonathon followed as Hans led them out of the parklike grounds in front of the church and into the unfamiliar streets. They emerged on the Ringstrasse and Hans led them farther, toward the center of town, through old neighborhoods and down commercial streets, until they emerged in the central square again. "You choose where you'd like to eat." Hans looked at him questioningly, and Jonathon nodded his head. "It's my treat, so choose anywhere you'd like." He made an expansive gesture, and Hans grinned, turning toward a café with tables and umbrellas set outside.

Seated by a starchily dressed maître d', Jonathon took the offered menu, unsure of what the man was saying, but Hans gave instructions, and the imposing man nodded briskly before walking away. Jonathon decided it was probably best to let Hans handle things, so he looked around, watching people and enjoying the slower, less hurried pace. A waiter stopped by, and they placed their order, with Jonathon thankful the menu had rudimentary English translations. He'd been to Germany years before, so the food wasn't completely strange, and he did his best not to butcher the German names of the dishes. "So, how much more school do you have?" Jonathon asked once the waiter had left.

"Three weeks, then I'm on holiday for a month before I start at the university. I'm lucky because I will stay here in Wien."

"Aren't you young to be attending university?"

Hans nodded and smiled proudly. "I finished what you call high school a year early, so I will be younger than most of my colleagues." The waiter returned, bringing a large beer for each of them. Jonathon almost said something, but then remembered that Hans was legal to drink. Just another reminder of how different things were in Europe.

"I know you want to be an art restorer. Do you know how long you will need to study?"

Hans took a gulp of his beer before answering, wiping the froth off his lips. "At least six years so I can do what I want. Oma and Mutti say they will help all they can. After I graduate, I will still have to perform my military service, but then I will maybe get a better assignment." The conversation trailed off when the server brought the salad course, and Hans began eating as though he were starved. Jonathon ate as well, taking his time, watching everything going on.

The main courses came and were eaten, followed by a pair of chocolate mousse desserts. By the time they were done, Jonathon felt stuffed and ready for the walk home.

Hans kept up a running commentary as they made their way through the city streets, past the opera house, where Jonathon bought tickets for later in the week. A moment of melancholy fell over him when he realized that he'd bought two out of habit. Continuing down Operngasse, the two men turned onto their small street. Just around the main corner, Jonathon saw the thin youngster standing at the corner near the house, on the far side of the street, selling himself to passersby. Jonathon raised his hand, and the waif raised in his hand in response, smiling slightly before turning his attention to potential customers.

As they approached, Jonathon heard Hans huff and then run across the street to where a car had stopped in front of the boy. Hans began to yell something in German, and the car sped away, peeling rubber as it did. Hans continued yelling, and the boy stumbled and fell as Fabian came out of the house, seeing Hans and running over. "Hans, it's okay, leave him alone."

Accompanied by a Waltz

Fabian reached his brother at the same time Jonathon did. Fabian pulled Hans away, trying to calm his brother down. "Are you okay?" Jonathon asked, helping the boy back to his feet.

"Yes," he replied haltingly in English, brushing himself off. Fabian led Hans back toward the house, and the street quieted.

"Why don't you work another corner? Because I don't think he's going to leave you alone."

"I can't," he said as another car slowed and then sped away. The kid's eyes followed the car with a look of despair, and Jonathon found himself digging into his pockets, pulling out some bills before pressing them into a slender hand and walking away.

As he approached the house, Jonathon saw Fabian standing on the sidewalk, watching him. "Why did you do that? Why did you give him money?"

Jonathon hesitated before answering, studying Fabian, realizing his tone wasn't accusatory, even though he wasn't sure what it was. "There but by the grace of God," was Jonathon's only response as he turned away and made his way through the still car-filled courtyard, into his apartment, and up the circular staircase.

Seeing Greg's picture, Jonathon fell onto the bed, staring into that familiar, smiling face. For the first time he could remember since Greg's death, he'd gone hours without thinking about him. He and Hans had had a great time in the city, and he'd loved the time he'd spent with his young friend. But now Jonathon could feel his unhappy past, a past long before Greg, starting to rear its ugly head. Picking up the picture, he once again stared into that loving face. "I never knew why you loved me, but you did." Putting the picture back, he forced himself off the bed. He had to move on. He couldn't let himself be defined by his past, either the happy one with Greg, or the years before that he'd worked so hard to forget—that Greg had helped him forget. Walking down the stairs, he stepped out on the small balcony, chin resting against his hands, watching the now-quiet street.

CHAPTER Five

THE next few days were blessedly and relaxingly quiet. Jonathon spent part of his days wandering the city, and he'd even found a fantastic bookstore with an extensive English language selection, so he'd spent time just sitting on his balcony in the chair he'd bought and dragged home, reading and enjoying the quiet. Occasionally, he'd look up from his book as conversation or other sounds from the street intruded, but otherwise he read contentedly.

Tuesday afternoon found him quietly reading, feet up on a stool he'd dragged out, a cool drink on a small table. With a yawn, Jonathon found himself closing his eyes, ready for a short afternoon nap, the book resting open on his lap. Sinking into the chair, he drifted into a light doze.

A sound invaded his peace, one that definitely didn't belong. At first he wasn't sure he'd heard it, but it repeated, and without thinking he stood up, his book hitting the floor as he looked over the wall toward the street. There it was again, and this time he was sure it was the sound of someone being hit, followed by words he didn't understand, but the tone, a combination of fear, near-panic, and pleading, sent Jonathon racing through the house and out his door, weaving through the courtyard and out onto the sidewalk. "What are you doing?" he yelled as he saw a large man holding someone who looked like the young man Hans kept chasing away, dragging him into a narrow passageway between two buildings. "Let him go or I'll call the police!" Jonathon yelled, hoping the men understood English. Jonathon kept yelling, seeing doors open and a few people stepping out onto the sidewalk.

Looking around, not sure what he should do, he saw Fabian rushing up the sidewalk, the door to the house left open. "What is it, Jonathon? What's going on?"

"Someone's being attacked," Jonathon said, pointing toward the passageway, following Fabian as he peered between the buildings. He heard him gasp.

Without thinking, Jonathon hurried around the corner. The young man lay crumpled against the side of the building, blood staining his shirt, the red patch growing larger. "Get me something I can use to stop the bleeding and call an ambulance," Jonathon yelled to Fabian, who just stood there, looking down at the boy without moving. "Fabian, go!" Jonathon shook Fabian's shoulder, and he seemed to come back to himself, nodding and hurrying away.

Taking off his shirt, he bunched it in his hand, placing the fabric over the wound, pressing hard. Fabian returned with a white cloth, and Jonathon replaced his soaked shirt with the cloth, pressing down. "I called emergency services," Fabian said as he knelt next to him. "Is he going to be okay?" Jonathon looked at the boy's pale complexion and closed eyes, shrugging his answer. He just didn't know.

Finally, after what seemed like an eternity, Jonathon heard the two-tone wail of sirens that got louder and louder before stopping nearby. Footsteps rushed toward them, and instructions were barked at him that he didn't understand. "Speak English, for God's sake!" Jonathon's patience was running thin.

One of the men placed his hand on the makeshift bandage, and Jonathon let go, stepping back, watching as the men did their job. For a second, as Jonathon watched, it wasn't the boy, but Greg. "Not again," he whispered to himself, clamping his eyes closed to stop the impending tears.

"Jonathon," Fabian said from behind him, a hand touching his arm. "We should get out of their way."

Jonathon walked to the man who was standing back. He seemed to be in charge. "Is he going to be okay?"

"I think we got here in time," was the only answer Jonathon got as more sirens sounded. The police arrived, taking charge and asking questions. Jonathon told them what he could, describing the man he'd seen to the best of his ability, and after being dismissed by the police, he walked back toward the house with Fabian next to him.

"Thank you for helping," Jonathon told Fabian blankly as he walked between the cars to his door.

"Are you feeling well? You look a little white."

Jonathon went inside, sitting on one of the dining room chairs, half-watching as Fabian searched through the cupboards, coming up with a bottle. Pouring the amber liquid into a glass, Fabian handed it to him, and Jonathon drank it without thinking, first coughing at the unexpected bite before downing the rest in a gulp. "Thank you. What was that?"

"Brandy. I'm surprised it's still here," Fabian said as he poured a second glass. "Would you like to be alone? I can go." Gulping, he emptied the glass, setting it in the sink.

Jonathon shook his head. "No, please." He motioned toward the stairs and followed Fabian up to the living room. "I hope he'll be okay," Jonathon said as he sat in one of the chairs.

"Can I ask something?"

Jonathon nodded in response.

"He was only a Strichjunge. Were you involved with him? Were you a customer? I saw you give him money. It is okay if you were... I do not mean to judge."

"No, I wasn't a customer, and no, Fabian, he wasn't *just* a Strichjunge. He was a human being, a person." Jonathon swallowed, his emotions dangerously close to the surface. "Just because he sold himself to survive doesn't mean he was any less a person or any less valuable than anyone else!" Jonathon found himself yelling and tried to calm himself down. "I'm sorry, I shouldn't have yelled." Looking up, he saw a warmth in those brown eyes he hadn't expected, and his frustration evaporated.

"No, I am the one who is sorry. I should not judge, I know how it feels." Fabian's voice became quiet, those dark eyes deep and touched with sorrow. "Do you want to lie down? You look tired?"

"No, I'm all right." Jonathon settled in his chair, sighing softly. "It's just that a long time ago, when I was young and alone… I was a Strichjunge, and I know how it feels to be treated as though you're nothing." Jonathon closed his eyes and felt his voice trail off as his memory bombarded him with things he'd forgotten for so many years. The helplessness, the need to escape but having no place to go, all flooded through his mind, and he found himself shivering as though the room had suddenly gotten cold.

"Jonathon, you don't have to talk about this if you don't want to, but I'll listen if you want," Fabian said quietly, and Jonathon lifted his eyes. He expected to see pity or worse, but all he saw in Fabian's deep brown eyes was compassion, tinged with sadness.

"You don't need to sit here and listen to me tell sob stories." Jonathon looked toward the open balcony door, his mind already carrying him back to the past. "I'm just oversensitive right now. It'll pass." A hand touched his, and Jonathon turned, finding himself looking into Fabian's eyes, and he felt the rings around his heart, the ones that had clamped into place when Greg died, begin to loosen.

"Tell me your story, Jonathon," Fabian whispered very softly. "I want to hear it."

"Why?" Jonathon responded, caught up in those eyes for a second. Then he turned away, looking anywhere but at Fabian. "Why could you possibly be interested?" Jonathon felt Fabian's fingers ghost across the back of his hands, stroking softly. He opened his mouth, fully intending to ask Fabian to go, but instead he began talking quietly. "I was sixteen when my parents died in an automobile accident. Unfortunately, since they were both only children, I had no other relatives, and I was sent to a foster home." Jonathon still felt the loneliness and heartbreak at the loss of his parents as though it were yesterday, with loss piling on top of loss. "I didn't stay long and ran away. That was my first mistake."

"Were they cruel?"

Jonathon shook his head slowly. "No, they just weren't my parents, and in my stupidity, I thought I would be better off on my own. I found out differently. It wasn't long until I was hungry, searching for food anywhere I could find it. Eventually, I found out I could make money selling myself on the streets of New York." Jonathon swallowed hard. "I was so freaking lucky I didn't get some disease." He looked out the window again. "Or worse," he added, thinking of the boy bleeding on the concrete. "I got rescued from the streets, anyway, by an old priest who found me and helped me. Father Joda ran a school and gave me a home there and a chance at an education."

Jonathon felt his eyes watering, and he wiped them on the back of his hand. He hadn't told this story to anyone since he'd told it to Greg, years before. "He was a special man, and I thought he loved me, but he didn't, not really." Jonathon wondered if he should go on. He knew Fabian's family was Catholic, and he didn't want to offend them, so he fell quiet, listening to the sounds of the city as they floated through the window.

"Let me guess," Fabian prompted. "Someone found out about your past?"

Jonathon nodded. "One of the instructors, a young priest, found out what I'd done before I came to the school, and he took advantage. At first I said nothing, but eventually I told Father Joda, and he didn't believe me." Jonathon took measured, deep breaths, reminding himself that this had all happened a long time ago and had nothing to do with the person he was now.

Fabian's fingers continued rubbing his hands. "What did you do?"

"For a while I took it, figuring it was my fault anyway. Once I graduated, some other boys came forward as well, and Father Joda finally listened to me. He helped me get into college, where I decided to become a teacher so I could help make sure no other child went through what I did." Jonathon stopped talking, figuring he'd said more than enough. He wasn't proud of his past, but Greg had helped him realize that while it was part of who he was, it didn't define him.

"So that's why you gave the Strichjunge money."

"I figured he'd get in trouble if he didn't bring in enough money, and I guess I was right." Jonathon sighed. "I know I can't help everyone, but I wish I could have done more for him. He certainly didn't deserve the treatment he got either from Hans or the man who nearly killed him." Jonathon knew it would be hard for Fabian to understand, and he really didn't have any hope that he really would, but at least he'd told his side.

"You're a kind man, Jonathon," Fabian said as he leaned closer, so close Jonathon could feel his warmth, smell his minty breath, the scent of his skin clouding his mind with feelings and desire he wasn't sure he was ready to feel yet. Fabian leaned closer still, lips parting slightly. Jonathon shook himself out of his daze, getting to his feet and walking to the other side of the room, needing to put some distance between himself and the beautiful man now kneeling in front of an empty chair.

"I can't, Fabian," he said breathlessly, trying to gain control of his traitorous body.

"Why not?" Fabian replied as he got to his feet, slowly moving closer. "You're kind and thoughtful, smart, and very attractive."

"Because it wouldn't be right." Jonathon turned away. "I think you should go." He jumped when he felt a hand on his shoulder, and he almost brushed it off, but instead he hugged his arms around himself.

"Why wouldn't it be right?" Fabian asked, and Jonathon could feel him, knew exactly where he was like he could see him. His skin seemed to want to reach out to him, and that scared Jonathon. "There isn't someone else, is there?"

Jonathon didn't know how to answer that question. How could he tell Fabian that there was, sort of, but that he was dead? Even in his mind it sounded creepy. "No, at least not in the way you mean."

The hand slipped off his shoulder. "Okay, I'll go, but will you do something for me? Will you have dinner with me?"

"Why?" Jonathon whispered to the wall. "Why would you want to have dinner with me? I'm old and brokenhearted. What could I have that could interest you?"

"Your heart is not broken, Jonathon," Fabian breathed softly behind him. "It's kind and gentle and beautiful, just like the rest of you." He felt the light touch of what he thought were Fabian's lips on his neck, so softly he couldn't really be sure it had happened.

Jonathon whirled around, locking eyes with Fabian. "Do you know how that sounds?" Challenging Fabian to see if he was being handed a line, all Jonathon saw was a sincere softness in those sparkling eyes, and an unexpected innocence. It would have been easy to dismiss Fabian as a player, with his big eyes, movie-star looks, and shining raven hair that almost screamed for Jonathon to run his fingers through it, but he couldn't. This man surprised him, and he'd like to think that was hard to do, particularly after his youth, but… that was a long time ago.

"I have tickets for the opera on Thursday. We could get dinner before if you want." God, Jonathon sincerely hoped he wasn't going to regret this. He'd have to make sure he didn't regret it. They'd have dinner, see the opera, and that was all. Afterwards, he'd come back to his apartment, and Fabian would go home as well. It was that simple.

At least it seemed that way until Fabian smiled and leaned forward, touching his lips ever so softly. "Then I'll leave you until Thursday." With a smoldering smile, Fabian turned and walked toward the stairs, descending until just his torso could be seen. He saw Fabian stop and felt the heated gaze as it traveled up his body, and Jonathon felt a small shiver run up his spine. Then Fabian stepped lower, and Jonathon watched as he disappeared and continued watching the stairs where he'd disappeared until he heard the door thud closed.

Gasping for breath, he stood immobile for a long while, wondering what had just happened, and more importantly, how he could have let it happen. He knew it was stupid for him to feel as though having dinner with Fabian was somehow being unfaithful to Greg, but that was it, and he knew it. Walking up the stairs, he found himself looking at the photograph by the bed. He knew exactly what Greg would say and scoffed at himself. "You'd kick my ass if you knew how I was acting, wouldn't you?" Greg would want him to move on, and he'd definitely want him to be happy. Jonathon didn't know exactly what would make him happy, but there was one thing he knew: sitting on his balcony for the next two months reading books while the world went by wasn't going to do it. And neither was pining for a lover, friend, and partner who was gone. It was time to live again.

As Jonathon put the picture back on the nightstand, his phone rang, and he dug it out of his pocket, smiling when he saw the caller. "Jeana, how are you? Where are you?"

He heard a carefree laugh. "We're in Innsbruck, and we'll be heading to Vienna in a few days so we can see our families before pressing on. How are you? Is the apartment nice? Are you meeting people?" She peppered him with questions, and Jonathon tried to answer them.

"I'm fine. The apartment's really nice, perfect for me, as a matter of fact, and yes, I've met Inge's family, they're very nice." He left out the part about the day's earlier excitement.

"Have you met anyone else?" she asked, and Jonathon could hear the expectation in her voice.

"Jeana." He resorted to his teacher voice.

"Okay. Inge and I will be there Thursday afternoon, and we can go to dinner."

Jonathon swallowed. "Um, I already have plans for Thursday evening." He knew there was no way she was going to let that slide.

"What kind of plans? Is he cute?"

"Jeana." Damn it, even the teacher voice was failing him. "I'm going to dinner with Fabian, Inge's cousin, and then we're going to the opera." He held the phone at arm's length as a squeal shot through the phone. "That's quite enough, young lady," he scolded when he was sure she wouldn't split his eardrums.

"Inge showed me pictures of her cousins—you sure know how to pick them, Dad. He's hot," she said, before clarifying, "for a guy."

Jonathon couldn't hold back his chuckle. "It's just dinner and the opera. So don't go picking out the wedding invitations or designing the floral arrangements just yet."

"Dad, I'm a lesbian. We didn't get the flower arrangement or etiquette genes, we got the Harley genes, remember?" She made a "sheesh" sound, and Jonathon doubled over with laughter, since neither of them fit either stereotype. "Well, if Thursday's out, then we can go to lunch on Friday and see some things. Inge's told me all about the Schönbrunn Palace. We're just spending a couple of days, and then we're off to Venice."

"Will you be back before classes start?"

"Yeah, we figure we'll be back in Vienna just before you leave for home." She sounded so excited, and Jonathon let himself soak up part of what came through the phone. "I'll see you in a few days."

They said their good-byes and Jonathon hung up, feeling a little excited about Thursday. Putting the phone next to Greg's picture, he opened the wardrobe, looking at the clothes he'd brought along.

Plain and boring—that was how he'd describe everything he had. Closing the wardrobe door, he looked around, scooping up his phone and wallet before grabbing his keys—it looked as though it was time to do a little shopping.

JONATHON heard Jeana before he saw her, but it wasn't long before his daughter's body caught up with her voice and he heard a knock on his door. Opening it, Jonathon was immediately engulfed in a hug that nearly knocked him off his feet amid squeals that made him wonder if he'd actually be able to hear the opera later that evening. Then she stood back, looking him over. "You look good, Dad."

"Thanks, sweetheart." Jonathon kissed her on the cheek. "So do you. Love must agree with you." Jonathon stepped back so Jeana could enter, and he closed the door before leading her up the stairs.

"Ooh, this place is really cozy. And even nicer than Inge told me," Jeana said as she sat in one of the chairs. "So tell me about this date you have tonight."

"It's not a date. Fabian and I are going to dinner and the opera. That's all."

Jeana's eyes widened. "So have you decided what you're wearing, or do I need to take you shopping?"

Jonathon couldn't help smiling. "I went shopping earlier in the week."

"I knew it." Jeana jumped to her feet. "This isn't a date, but you bought new clothes and look as though you're about ready to jump out of your skin. You keep telling yourself this isn't a date and maybe you'll start to believe it, because I sure as shit don't."

"Jeana, language."

"You're not going to distract me that easily. I'm not five anymore. Let's go see these clothes. Is the bedroom up there?" Jonathon nodded his response and Jeana was off like a shot, up the stairs before Jonathon had a chance to stand up. "You coming?" she called down. "Or do I get to find them myself?"

"I'm coming." Jonathon began climbing the stairs. "You're just like your father."

"I'll take that as a good thing," she responded, sitting on the edge of the bed, waiting for him. "Now let's see them."

Jonathon opened the wardrobe, taking out the pants and shirt, still wrapped in tissue paper, opening them before laying the clothes on the bed. "I wasn't sure where to go, but I found a really nice shopping area." He ran his hands over the soft shirt.

Jeana picked up the shirt, holding it in front of him. "I'll say you did." She grinned. "This is incredible silk, and the pants"—she picked them up, stroking the fabric—"are perfect for you." She handed them to him. "Go try them on, I want to see."

"Jeana, I'm not a child."

"When it comes to fashion, you are. So go try them on."

He could never tell her no, especially when she looked at him with that huge grin on her face. "Just turn around." She did, and Jonathon slipped off his shoes and lowered his pants before stepping into the new ones, the luxurious fabric sliding sensually along his legs. Slipping off his shirt, he pulled on the new silk shirt, buttoning it before tucking the tails into his pants. "So, what do you think?"

Jeana stood back. "Turn around." She made a little twirly motion with her hands, and Jonathon obediently turned around so she could see the back.

"I didn't want anything too flashy. I figured we were going to the opera, so I went rather traditional."

"You look stunning, Dad. And you made a good choice. The dark-gray slacks and white shirt are perfect."

Jonathon padded to the wardrobe in his stocking feet. "The lady at the shop also helped me pick out a belt and socks."

"I'll bet she did," Jeana said with a grin. "You probably made her sales week. Seriously, Dad, does this mean when we're back in New York, you'll let me take you shopping? These are expensive clothes, and they look so good on you." She fingered the silk of the shirt, adjusting his collar. "You deserve to wear clothes like this. I'm surprised Dad didn't buy them for you."

"Your father would have bought me wardrobes full of clothes if I'd let him. But I didn't, and now I wish I had." Jonathon sat on the edge of the bed. "Not that I wanted them, but because it would have made him happy."

"What made Daddy happy was what made you happy. That man loved you more than anything or anyone on earth, including us." Jonathon hurried to her, hugging Jeana tight as she began tearing up. "I'm not upset or jealous, because he should have. You were his other half, and with the way I feel about Inge, I'm really starting to understand just what you and Daddy had, and I want that too."

"You deserve it." Jonathon held her, and to his surprise, he found that his eyes were dry and he was able to smile. "Everyone deserves to find that kind of love once in their life. I'm lucky I had it with your father. I didn't get to keep him as long as I'd hoped, but I wouldn't trade a minute for anything in the world." Jonathon could feel Greg's love warming him from the inside.

"So you're going to have fun on your date tonight?" Jeana asked as she wiped her eyes, pulling out of the embrace.

"Yeah, I am." Jonathon felt his cheeks heat. "I haven't been out with anyone since Greg, and I'm a little nervous."

"Don't be," Jeana reassured him. "Just do what you told me when I went on my first date, remember?"

Jonathon smiled at the memory. "Be yourself, and if the boy tries anything"—Jonathon grinned—"go for the jewels," they finished together, laughing like idiots.

"So what time is your date?"

Jonathon checked his watch. "We're supposed to meet in an hour."

"Then you'd better get ready." Jeana walked toward the stairs. "I'm going to find Inge, but I'll be back in forty-five minutes to check you out before he gets here." She started down the stairs, and Jonathon shook his head, stripping off his clothes and laying them on the bed before heading to the bathroom.

After cleaning up and dressing, Jonathon found himself pacing the living area nervously, a million questions racing through his mind. What if Fabian didn't really like opera and was bored through the whole thing? Were they coming back here afterwards? He'd made sure everything was clean just in case. Would Fabian kiss him again? That was the one question he kind of hoped would be a yes. It had felt nice when Fabian kissed him, and it made him feel desired again. But that led to the next question: what if Fabian wanted more? That one really got his heart pounding, and he wasn't sure if it was a good thing or not. He'd been alone for the last two years, and he hadn't even looked at another man, feeling as though he was being unfaithful to Greg. He was still young, well, relatively young anyway, and the thought of seeing that rich skin again, wondering what it would feel like to touch and be touched, had his body racing.

It wasn't as though he didn't know what to do, and Greg was gone, he knew that. And he needed to move on. But he hadn't been with anyone other than Greg in almost two decades. He'd gotten a good look at himself in the mirror, and in the immortal words of Dolly Parton, "Time marches on, and eventually you find it's marching across your face." And in his case, the rest of him as well. *You're worrying about something that probably won't happen anyway.*

A knock sounded from the door, and Jonathon had never been so grateful for the interruption. He let Jeana inside, and she immediately looked him over. "Nice, Dad, very nice," she said with a smile.

"Thank you." Jonathon peered outside before closing the door. "I'm so nervous."

"Don't be, Dad. It's dinner and the opera, just like you said. I know I was teasing you earlier, but just be yourself and have a good time." She reached up and adjusted his collar. "If it's any consolation, he's just as nervous as you are."

"I don't think that's possible."

"Oh yeah." Jeana's eyes sparkled with mischief. "He's been running around upstairs and has changed his clothes at least three times." Jeana began to chuckle. "And all under the eye of his grandmother, who watches him like a hawk. That woman is a real piece of work. Inge's Aunt Hanna seems like a lot of fun, I just love her. But the grandmother is one old-fashioned woman with old-fashioned notions and bigotries."

"I was forewarned by Hanna when I moved in." Jonathon looked toward the main house, and Jeana turned him around, making sure his collar and shirt were perfect all around before pronouncing him presentable.

"I don't know what Fabian did to piss off his grandmother, but whatever it was, she hasn't forgiven him. She keeps trying to keep an eye on him, and Hanna keeps giving her things to keep her busy in another part of the house. Add in Hans scowling at his brother because he told him he couldn't come along and it's like a sitcom in there."

Jonathon sat in one of the chairs. "Are you going to be here when I get back?"

Jeana looked horrified. "Not on your life. So feel free to bring Fabian back here and have your way with him."

"Jeana! Do you know how icky it is to think of your parents having sex?" Jeana nodded with a mock-shiver. "Well, it's just as icky talking about your sex life with your kids."

"Okay, I'm going to find Inge so she and I can paint the town red." She hugged him tightly. "You have a great time, and don't order anything drippy or messy during dinner." With those parting words she was gone, and Jonathon grinned, watching her as she walked past the window. Checking his watch, Jonathon hurried upstairs, going to the wardrobe and getting his light jacket before returning to the living room level to wait.

As he did, voices traveled through the open window, and Jonathon wandered out onto the balcony. He saw Fabian and Jeana standing together in the unusually empty courtyard, their voices drifting. He couldn't make out what they were saying, but they parted, and Jeana walked toward the main house. Jonathon headed downstairs, walking to the door as Fabian knocked. "Right on time," Jonathon commented with a wide smile.

"I would have been here earlier, but Jeana caught me on my way over."

"I can just imagine," Jonathon replied. "Shall we go?"

"I thought we'd walk, if that's okay. The restaurant is between here and the opera house. It's just a few blocks."

"Lead the way." Jonathon expected them to leave, but he found himself engulfed in a pair of strong arms and saw Fabian tilt his head just before their lips touched in a kiss that nearly made his knees buckle, not from the heat, but from the caged desire he could feel being held at bay. That those feelings seemed to be for him was heady, and when the kiss deepened slightly, Jonathon let Fabian carry them where he wanted to go.

Footsteps in the courtyard seemed to startle Fabian, and he ended the kiss, stepping away before smiling. Fabian motioned to the door. Jonathon picked up his jacket from the floor, where he'd dropped it during the kiss, and stepped outside, seeing Oma walking their way. Jonathon waved to her innocently, smiling at the old woman as he walked toward the street. She waved back at him but stared at Fabian as they opened the iron gate and stepped onto the nearly deserted sidewalk, the gate clanging closed behind them. "The restaurant is this way. You've probably walked past a few times already. It's not very big, but the food...." He kissed his fingers dramatically. "And it's owned by a friend of mine."

They walked side by side, with Fabian's hand brushing against his every few seconds, the touch seeming illicitly naughty. Approaching the restaurant, Jonathon saw a few tables on the sidewalk surrounded by fencing draped with fairy lights. He hoped they were going to sit there, but Fabian led them inside, speaking to the hostess in German. She left and returned with a man who greeted Fabian warmly. "This is the man you were telling me about." He extended his hand.

"Jonathon, this is Heinrich, he's the owner and the best chef in all of Vienna," Fabian replied, and they shook hands. Then Heinrich led them toward the back and to a secluded table. He and Fabian spoke in German very briefly, and then Heinrich left with a smile. "We were young together."

"I take it he knows about you?"

Fabian laughed. "Most people know I like men."

"Everyone except Oma?" Jonathon was sure she knew—or suspected.

Fabian's laugh faded away. "Oma knows. She's just stuck in the past and will not accept it."

A server brought a bottle of wine, showing it to Fabian and him, and after getting approval, he popped the cork and gave Fabian a taste before pouring for both of them. Once he'd left, Fabian lifted his glass, and they toasted silently, clinking glasses before tasting the wine. "A while ago, when I was living in the apartment, Oma came in, she said to clean, but she was just being... nosey?" Fabian questioned the use of the term, and Jonathon nodded and smiled. "She found me in the living room with my boyfriend."

"That must have been a shock for her." It would be for almost anybody.

"She screamed at him and started calling him nasty things and he left, really fast. That is why Hans hates the Strichjunge so much. Oma called Phillipe that in front of him, and Hans took it literally." Fabian took another drink of his wine. "After that, she told me no more men or I have to leave. So I left."

That explained Hans's hostility—he blamed them for the loss of his brother. "Is that why she keeps watching you?" Fabian looked surprised, and Jonathon explained, "Jeana told me before you came that she kept looking for you all the time."

"Yes, she tells me all the time that I need a wife to get married. She will listen to nothing else. That was why she watched when we left tonight. The bad thing is that she owns the house, so I may have to leave again soon," Fabian said with a touch of sadness.

The thought of Fabian leaving sent a rush through Jonathon, and he had to stop and make himself think. He'd only known Fabian for a few days, but the idea of him leaving made him anxious.

"Do not worry, I will not leave soon. If I find a job, then I can get my own apartment, away from Oma." He grinned.

"What kind of job do you do?"

"For work, I draw buildings for architects." He pronounced the "ch," and Jonathon thought it was adorable and smiled without correcting him. "I want to design my own buildings someday, but for now I have to pay my dues, I think you'd say."

The server stopped by their table, and Fabian ordered starters as Jonathon scanned over the menu before putting it down again. "I'll trust you to order for me," Jonathon said, grateful that Fabian's attention seemed to be shifting from Oma.

Fabian nodded and looked over his menu and then set it down. Reaching across the table, Fabian took his hand, thumbs slipping over his skin. Jonathon looked into beautiful eyes, big and dark, waiting for Fabian to say something, but he didn't, at least not with his lips. But his eyes deepened, the gentle touch became more urgent as ripples of energy passed between them. Jonathon had never known such intimacy and intensity from so simple a gesture. The server returned, setting down a plate in front of each of them, then leaving again, and Fabian didn't look away, not for a second. Jonathon knew if he had, the spell would have broken, but Fabian's gaze on him felt like a magnet, and he couldn't turn away from it. He needed it the way a flower needs the rain after a week of summer heat.

Slowly, Fabian's hands slipped away, and everything around him came back into focus. The conversations from other tables reached his ears, and the movement of waiters caught his attention again, if only briefly. Looking down, he saw a dish with small depressions, each filled with butter, smelling of garlic and herbs. "Are these escargot?" He'd half expected Fabian to order oysters.

Fabian nodded and used a tiny fork to spear one, and Jonathon did the same, the morsel sensually sliding down his throat, flavor bursting onto his tongue. Taking a sip of wine, he speared another, eating slowly, savoring every bite as well as the company. The first course was followed by their entrees of duck in a sauce that smelled like heaven and tasted even better. They talked very little, which was a surprise to Jonathon, but whenever he looked up, he saw Fabian looking at him, fork still, his meal ignored.

Accompanied by a Waltz

"What are we seeing this evening?" Fabian asked, breaking a long, gaze-filled silence.

"*La Bohême*. I saw it once, years ago." Jonathon chuckled at the memory. "It made me cry, if I remember."

"See," Fabian smiled triumphantly. "I said you had a gentle heart, and I was right." The server cleared their plates and inquired about dessert, but they declined, and Jonathon assumed Fabian told him to bring the check right away, because he hurried away and returned, placing the leather folder on the table. Fabian reached for it, but Jonathon was quicker, pulling out a card and placing it in the folder.

"This evening is mine, Fabian." The server took it and returned so Jonathon could sign the slip. After saying good night to Fabian's friend, they walked through the lamplit streets toward the opera house. This time, Fabian's hand found his, the night and the shadows acting as disguise.

JONATHON wiped his eyes as the curtain fell on the last act of the opera. The heroine had died, just like he had known she would, but it didn't seem to help his emotions much. The curtain rose again and the audience also rose to their feet, thunderous applause filling the ornate auditorium from the gilded ornamentation and crystal chandeliers to the royal box above their heads. Then, after the performers had taken their bows and Jonathon's hands ached from applauding so long and hard, the heavily decorated curtain, itself a work of art, closed for the last time. Sitting back down, Jonathon waited for the crowd to thin. "I always wanted to see a performance here." He purposely left out any reference to Greg. On their way from the restaurant, he realized how much he'd been comparing Fabian and everything they did to what he and Greg had done. And that wasn't fair. Fabian was his own person and deserved to be seen as such. Jonathon knew how he'd feel if he were constantly compared to someone else.

"Was it worth the wait?" Fabian asked, nudging his shoulder.

Jonathon grinned widely as he nudged Fabian back. "It was so worth it." Standing up, he took a final look around the spectacular building before walking toward the exit.

"I thought we'd get a bite of dessert before we head back," Fabian said from behind him.

"Are places still open?" He automatically checked his watch. "It's quite late."

"Of course, if you know where to look," Fabian answered with a wink, and they stepped out into the crisp evening air. The brightly lit opera house faded in the distance as they crossed the street, walking back toward home. To Jonathon's confusion, they didn't stop anywhere and arrived at the gate a while later, but Fabian led them to his door and waited until he opened it.

Turning on the light, he saw a pastry box sitting on the counter. "What did you do?"

"I asked Jeana to bring something back for us."

"You sneak," Jonathon snipped lightly before picking up the box. "What would you like to drink? I have a dessert wine, if you're up for it."

"Of course." Fabian stepped closer, and Jonathon couldn't stop the kiss, with his hands full—not that he wanted to anyway. "I'll meet you upstairs." Fabian took the pastry box, carrying it up the stairs. Jonathon got the wine and opened it, carrying the bottle and two glasses upstairs as well.

"So, what did you have Jeana get?" Jonathon poured the wine, setting the glasses on the table before sitting next to Fabian on the sofa, watching as he opened the box, the scent filling the room.

"I had her pick up finger pastries," Fabian answered as he lifted out a small éclair, bringing it to Jonathon's lips. Opening his mouth, Jonathon took the pastry, chewing on the luscious pâte à choux, cream, and chocolate concoction. "Good?" Fabian asked, and Jonathon nodded, lifting out another, holding it to Fabian's mouth. He sucked in the pastry along with giving Jonathon's fingers a lick with his tongue.

Instead of picking up another pastry, Fabian swallowed, leaning close, kissing Jonathon gently, lips exploring, tongue lightly tracing the edge of his mouth, before backing away again. It got to be a game as they fed each other and kissed, each tasting the dessert on the other's skin.

A box of pastries and half a bottle of wine later, Jonathon was being kissed within an inch of his life, pressed back against the cushions. He felt Fabian shift, guiding him onto his back, and a hand slid beneath his shirt, warm fingers gliding over his skin.

"Fabian, I can't," Jonathon said against Fabian's lips, his mind overcoming the sensations his body seemed to crave.

Fabian stopped, lifting his head, eyes imploring. "Did I do something wrong?"

"No." Jonathon sat back up, his hand touching Fabian's arm. "It's just too soon."

"I understand." Fabian moved away, body rigid.

"No, I don't think you do. I was with Greg for a long time, and only with him. You haven't done anything wrong," Jonathon added hastily, as he wondered what in the hell he was doing. Here was a young, handsome man, obviously ready to take him to bed, and he was putting on the brakes. "I can't have sex and not have it mean something. I've made love for a very long time, and I want that again."

"Oh." Fabian brightened, turning back to him with a smile on his face. "Then I just have to let you fall in love with me."

"Pretty sure of yourself, aren't you?" Jonathon quipped, but he quickly found himself back where he was before, lips kissing, a hard body pressing him into the cushions, a warm hand caressing his stomach, fingers lightly tweaking a nipple, and Jonathon moaned softly, returning the kiss, holding Fabian tight.

Then Fabian stopped, gentling the kiss, weight lifting off him, hands slipping away from his skin. "I have an appointment for a job in the morning, but in the afternoon, can I take you someplace special?"

Jonathon nodded absently, and then his brain kicked in. "Umm, I'm supposed to go to Schönbrunn with Jeana and Inge." He hated to say no, but he'd already promised, and he couldn't disappoint her.

"Perfect." Fabian leaned close, giving him another kiss before moving just out of kissing range. "That's just what I had in mind. Would you like some company of your own?"

"I'd like that," Jonathon responded, getting to his feet, straightening his clothes before leaning in for another kiss. "Then I'll see you tomorrow."

Fabian leaned in one last time, kissing him until he could barely think. "That will give you something special to remember when you're in your bed tonight." Fabian winked and walked to the stairs. "Schlaf gut." With another quick smile, Fabian descended. Jonathon heard the door close, and he walked up the stairs to the bedroom. Slipping out of his clothes, he placed them carefully in the wardrobe before cleaning up and sliding between the sheets. He could still feel Fabian's kiss as he fell asleep.

CHAPTER Six

Jonathon woke late and lay in bed, thinking of Fabian and what his hands felt like when they touched his skin. Getting up before he took himself in hand, he pulled on a pair of sweatpants and a T-shirt before walking down to the kitchen and making a pot of coffee. Standing around and waiting, he opened the refrigerator, reminding himself that he really needed to do some shopping. The aroma of fine coffee filled the kitchen, and Jonathon closed the door, inhaling deeply. When the pot was finally finished, he poured a large mug and climbed back to the living room, settling on the sofa and turning on the television.

There wasn't much on in English, but it really didn't seem to matter. Jonathon was only using it for the noise anyway. Hearing a soft rap at his door, he set the mug aside and walked downstairs to answer it.

He'd expected to see Jeana standing on his doorstep—what he didn't expect was Fabian and Hans's grandmother. Oma was carrying a small dish in her hands like a gift, but when she looked up at him, Jonathon shivered, her expression as cold as any he'd ever seen, made even more so by her tight bun and severe black dress. "Guten Morgen," he said in his best German. "Can I help you?" he asked, not quite sure what else to say.

She extended her hands, smiling slightly, offering the dish before motioning inside. Jonathon stepped back, taking the offered dish and letting her come inside. He offered her a cup of coffee and she seemed to accept, so Jonathon poured one for each of them, setting them on the small table. "I come," she said, each word accentuated, her accent extremely heavy, "to ask Fabian."

Jonathon cocked his head to the side, unsure what she really wanted to say.

"Fabian good boy," she said, and Jonathon nodded because it seemed like the thing to do. "Fabian need make babies." She seemed emphatic about the last part. "I go now." She stood up, giving Jonathon a no-nonsense look before walking toward the door. "Hans and Fabian good boys," she said as she opened the door, walking outside and closing it behind her. Jonathon remained seated in the chair, staring at the door, wondering what in the hell had just happened.

Finally getting up, he poured her untouched coffee in the sink, rinsing the cup before picking up his own. He had just reached the stairs when he heard another knock and the door opened. "Morning, Dad."

He turned around. "Morning, Jeana." She began opening the cupboard doors until she found the cups, pouring some coffee before following him upstairs.

"So, how'd it go last night?" She didn't even let him sit down before the questioning began. "Did you have a good time?"

"Yes, I did. We had a very nice dinner, and the opera was… special." He couldn't keep the color from rising in his face. "Thank you for leaving the nibbles, by the way."

"My pleasure." She grinned over her cup. "So, let's cut to the chase—did you get some last night?"

"Jeana, I thought we agreed that some things were off-limits." Jonathon set down his cup, trying to stare her down.

"Not going to work. I'm not a third-grader, and I don't need details because that's just creepy"—she smiled for a second—"but did you get any?"

"You have a one-track mind. And no, I didn't get any. He tried"—Jonathon covered his embarrassment behind his cup—"but that's not what I want."

"Did you at least—"

Jonathon cut her off by raising his hand. "I'm not going to talk about this anymore. Unless you're prepared to answer my questions about you and Inge, and I very seriously doubt that you are." He finished his coffee, setting the empty cup next to the cold one from earlier. "So, are we still on for Schönbrunn today? Fabian said he had an appointment this morning but said if we went this afternoon, he'd go with us. It seems he has something sort of special planned."

"Sure. If he gets home in time, we can go for lunch first." Jeana finished her coffee, setting the cup next to his. "Was Oma here earlier? I saw her coming back, muttering something in German about you not understanding anything."

"Yeah." Jonathon settled back in his chair. "I think she was warning me off her grandchildren. It seems they are both good boys and that Fabian needs to make babies. That fits with what Fabian told me last night." Jonathon had no intention of relating the information to her that Fabian had shared. "I need to finish getting dressed so I can be ready to go when Fabian gets back." He checked his watch, realizing it was later than he thought. "You can stay here if you'd like, I'm not kicking you out or anything."

"No." she stood up. "I need to see what Inge's up to." She gave him a hug that he returned warmly. "I'm glad you had a good time, and I'm happy he likes you." She released him and turned, walking down the stairs. "Oh, and you might want to wash the chocolate out of the sofa cushions. It seems you two had some fun with the desserts." She winked and hurried away before he could scowl at her.

Jonathon got his clothes together, carrying them to the bathroom. After a shower, he dressed and made sure he looked his best before moving to the small balcony to take in some sunshine. Grabbing his book, he settled in the chair and began to read.

"Hey, gorgeous." Jonathon jumped when he heard Fabian's voice. Looking up, he saw brown eyes and then a pair of sensual lips brushed over his. "Jeana let me in."

Jonathon set down his book, pulling Fabian down for another kiss until he remembered where they were and pulled away. "Sorry, but we can be seen from the street. It doesn't bother me, but you might not want the neighbors talking."

Fabian chuckled softly. "Good point. Are you ready to go? The ladies are waiting for us by the gate." Jonathon got up, following Fabian inside, and closed the door before getting his wallet, keys, and other essentials.

They met Inge and Jeana by the gate and began walking toward the subway. "Do you want to get lunch there, or eat first?" Fabian asked, and they all agreed that they weren't really hungry, so they decided to wait, and walked directly to the subway station for the ride to what used to be the edge of the city.

"This was the summer palace for the emperor or empress and their family. The Hofburg is the city palace," Fabian explained once they were on the train. "The grounds are beautiful and quite extensive, but they used to be even larger. What's there today is only a small percentage of the hunting forest that used to surround Schönbrunn."

"Is it still used today?" Jeana asked. "Does anyone still live there?"

Fabian smiled. "No one lives there now. Parts of the building are used for government offices, but they aren't the royal parts. There's no empire any longer, but the bureaucratic portions of the building are still used for government departments." The train stopped, and they got off, walking toward a large, cold, yellow building. "This is the government part of the palace," Fabian said as he led them into a large courtyard surrounded by parts of the building, with huge gates crested and decorated in gold. "We need to get our tickets for the tour, and then we can walk through the gardens." They stood in line and got tickets. They had an hour, so Fabian led them to one of the cafés, and they ate a light lunch.

At the correct time, they lined up and were escorted into the building and taken through eye-popping rooms with frescoed ceilings, gilded and decorated plaster, and a ballroom that looked almost the size of a football field, with huge crystal chandeliers hanging from a hand-painted ceiling. Stunning was the only word that came to mind as Jonathon craned his neck to see all the ceiling at once. "Absolutely stunning." At the end of the tour, the guide left them outside in the gardens, and Jonathon found himself looking all around at the manicured grounds with sculptures and fountains.

"During the war, the palace itself suffered little damage. A bomb fell through the ballroom ceiling and lodged in the floor but didn't explode." Fabian pointed to the top of the hill on the far edge of the grounds. "The Gloriette didn't fare as well, but has been restored."

Jonathon continued looking around until he heard music. "What's that?" Jonathon asked, looking for the source.

Fabian leaned close. "That's the surprise." Fabian practically vibrated. "Once a week, they have a small orchestra that plays here, with dancers." Jonathon listened to the beginning chords and rhythm of an unmistakable Strauss waltz. "They give lessons."

"Don't you have to pay?"

"More than that, you need reservations." Fabian smirked and winked. "I called yesterday and got the last two spots." He held out his hand. "Shall we dance?"

Jonathon felt his eyes widen. "Here? Us? Won't everyone be shocked?"

Fabian shook his head. "I specifically asked, and they said they get a lot of same-sex couples. The girl on the phone actually laughed about it. So, are you game?"

"To learn to waltz with you? Absolutely." Jonathon smiled as Fabian took his hand and led him off to the side to a small courtyard, where the orchestra played and men in tuxes and women in long formal dresses whirled around a raised dance floor. People stood nearby watching, and Fabian led them to where a small group of people had congregated.

"They'll start the lesson after they're done dancing, in a few minutes," Fabian said as they joined the group.

Jonathon watched the dancers until they were done, with the audience clapping and filing away. "Guten Tag, meine Damen und Herren, good afternoon, ladies and gentlemen. I'm Helmut, and I'll be your instructor this afternoon, along with my partner Greta. What we're going to do is demonstrate and teach you the basic steps of the Viennese waltz." He motioned with his hand, and the orchestra began to play, and the two of them flowed around the dance floor, accentuating the movement of their feet and bodies. "We'd like each couple to come out onto the dance floor, and we'll start by talking you through the steps."

Fabian took his hand, and Jonathon followed him out onto the dance floor. "Who's going to lead?" Jonathon asked with a wink.

"I will, but only because I'm taller. Besides, I already know how to waltz."

"So you just wanted to dance with me then?" Jonathon said as he felt Fabian's hand on his waist, and they followed the instructor, moving one step at a time through the dance. The instructor had them repeat the moves, and then the orchestra began to play. Couples began to move around the floor, a little clumsily, but they were doing it.

"Do you want to give it a try?" Fabian asked when Jonathon didn't move.

"You mean dance? Sure. Keep time, don't step on my feet, and follow along." Jonathon began swaying to the rhythm of the music and then stepped right into the dance, twirling Fabian around the floor, smiling at his partner's open-mouthed surprise.

"You didn't tell me you could dance," Fabian said as they danced by one of the other couples.

"You never asked," Jonathon replied with a smile as he guided them through the steps, looking into Fabian's eyes. "In college I had a roommate who needed to take dance lessons for her wedding, and we took them together. It was so much fun that we continued them for almost a year. The waltz was one of the things I learned."

"Obviously," Fabian retorted as the music ended, and Jonathon found himself pulled into a hug. "Dancing with you is really hot."

The instructor began giving instructions again, and they listened until the music started once more. This time the tempo was slower, the notes making longer lines, dictating smooth, flowing movement. Jonathon saw Jeana and Inge standing near the dance floor, watching them. Then Jonathon felt Fabian's gaze on him, and everything around them faded away. Nothing existed but him, Fabian, and the music, their bodies responding without words, the movement of one dictating the movement of the other.

"You're beautiful, you know that?" Fabian said softly, and Jonathon missed a step before he could catch himself. "Your eyes waltz when you're happy, and right now they're dancing more than we are." Fabian smiled and took up the lead, guiding Jonathon around the floor, bodies flowing, eyes locking, energy flowing between them wherever they touched.

"You're pretty fabulous yourself," Jonathon murmured as the music continued. "I can't believe you took me dancing."

"We aren't dancing—we're waltzing in the waltz capital of the world."

The song drifted to a close, and the orchestra began again, the familiar chords of Strauss's "Blue Danube" floating around them, through the tree limbs, and filling the courtyard. Jonathon smiled as Fabian put one hand on his hip and took his hand in the other as they swayed through the introduction before stepping off and into the waltz. Intricately, flowingly, Fabian guided them around the floor, eyes never straying from his, gaze intense and full, attention focused on him and him alone. Jonathon felt as though at that moment the entire world consisted of just two people, and in that moment he felt his resistance fade, and the last of those bands around his heart fell away. Suddenly, he felt light, the weight of Greg's death, the fight over his estate and will, the sorrow, the pain, the loneliness—all of that slipped away and it was just him and Fabian dancing in the Viennese sunshine.

The music faded and Fabian slowed them to a stop, and Jonathon looked around. All the other students, instructors, and bystanders watched them as they stepped off the dance floor, standing next to Inge and Jeana. "Well, ladies and gentlemen, it looks as though we had a pair of experts in our midst," the instructor said to the group before beginning the music once again and continuing the class.

"You looked great, Dad," Jeana said as she gave him a hug. "You both did."

"Thanks." Jonathon felt Fabian's hand on the small of his back, and he was guided away from the dance lesson and out toward the main gardens. "Are we going up there?" Jonathon asked, looking at the gold building on the hill.

"Of course. It has one of the best views in all of Vienna," Fabian answered.

Inge and Jeana began walking, staying close together, obviously enthralled with one another. "I'm so glad she's happy. They seem good for each other," Jonathon told Fabian as they walked along the wide garden path lined with flower beds that framed the large, formal palace gardens.

"They do." Fabian ran his hand along Jonathon's arm. "But what I want to know is, what is it that makes you happy?"

Jonathon didn't know how to answer that question. After Greg's death, he'd forgotten how to be happy and had spent his days merely existing. He hadn't considered what would bring him happiness because the one person who'd given him joy was now gone. The last few days had shown him that he could be happy again—joy was his to experience once again—but he wasn't quite sure how, and he felt he had to give an honest answer. "I don't know. It's been awhile since I was happy—since I've allowed myself to be happy."

Fabian looked at him in a very curious manner that Jonathon couldn't quite decipher. "I don't understand. How can you not know what makes you happy?" Jonathon didn't have an answer and just shrugged instead. "Your Greg must have been very special."

"He was," Jonathon answered softly. "He was the one person who loved me unconditionally, and that's very rare, or at least it has been for me." He still felt some of the loneliness, but talking about Greg didn't hurt or leave him torn up the way it always had in the past. "You would have liked him. He was fun, loved life, and knew how to live. I was lucky." Jonathon looked up toward where they were going. "You really don't want me to talk about Greg here, do you?"

Fabian stopped walking, letting Jeana and Inge get further ahead. "You can talk about whatever you like."

"Good." Jonathon smiled, relieved that the still-sad subject of Greg would be left alone for now. "Then let's talk about where you went while you were gone. You must have seen some fascinating places."

"Actually," Fabian's expression darkened slightly, "I spent much of the time in Innsbruck. I was able to find a job there, but then business slowed down and they had to cut back. Since I was the last one hired, that was me."

"How did the job search go this morning?" Jonathon asked as they began climbing the hill to the Neptune Fountain.

"I'm hopeful. They seemed to like me and were impressed with my work. They said they would call next week."

Stopping at the dramatic Neptune Fountain with its naked figures, seahorses, sprays, and waterfalls, Jonathon used the opportunity to take plenty of pictures of the palace and grounds, as well as of them. A pleasant woman from New Jersey agreed to take pictures of the four of them, and they stood in front of the fountain, mist wetting their backs slightly as she snapped the pictures. Taking back the camera, Jonathon thanked her, and they continued up the hill.

At the top, the Gloriette, with its colonnades and pillars, loomed over them. "This was built by the Empress Maria Theresa, and many think it was to celebrate a victory in war, but it wasn't. It was built mostly as decoration to finish off the palace grounds," Fabian explained. Jonathon turned around, looking down toward the palace and the city beyond. "Beautiful, isn't it?" Fabian stood next to him, an arm winding around his waist.

"Yes. Thank you for this. It was amazing fun." Jonathon almost leaned forward but stopped himself.

"Oh for Pete's sake," Jeana said from behind him. "Just kiss the man." Jonathon threw her a glare and then leaned to Fabian, kissing him softly and quickly.

Together, they wandered around, climbing to the roof to take in the view before heading down and back toward the palace. Then, leaving the palace behind, they made their way to the subway. "Inge and I are going into the city. Would you like to join us?"

Jonathon looked to Fabian before declining. "I think we're going to head back. You two have fun."

"Thanks," Inge said with a smile when Fabian and Jeana were out of earshot, obviously interested in spending some time alone with Jeana.

At the subway station, they parted ways and boarded their train, waving as Jeana and Inge stood on the platform, waiting for theirs. "I know I said this before, but danke schön for today, it was special," Jonathon said

"You're welcome." They rode quietly, the train speeding beneath the city. After getting off, they walked toward the apartment. As they got close, Jonathon stopped in front of the passage between the houses. Trash and even a few rags littered the stained concrete. Jonathon wasn't sure if those were from the other day or not, but he couldn't stop a shiver from running up his spine.

"Do you think it would be possible to find out how he's doing?" Jonathon turned, but Fabian's surprised expression made him take a step back. "What?"

"Jonathon, it's admirable that you want to help him, but this is a street person who makes his living selling himself. It's probably best if we don't get involved. You helped him when he needed it, and that is pretty amazing, but...."

Jonathon didn't stand around to hear what else Fabian had to say. Standing tall, he walked away, stopping only to open the gate before walking through the courtyard and into the apartment, closing the door. He made it as far as one of the dining chairs before his righteous indignation faded away, replaced by disappointment and hurt.

He should have known that things with Fabian were too good to be true. Granted, he'd probably overreacted, and Fabian's attitude was probably what he should have expected, but the look on Fabian's face had been so unemotional and cold. The thing was, Jonathon couldn't help putting himself in that young man's position because he knew what it felt like, and he knew he was lucky he hadn't ended up nearly bleeding to death in some alley somewhere himself. Standing up, he went upstairs, putting his camera away. He needed to get food for dinner, and now was as good a time as any.

Leaving the apartment, he didn't look around for Fabian but hurried out through the gate and down the street. Jonathon couldn't help glancing down the passageway again before hurrying on to the small market a few blocks away. Continuing on, he did his shopping and carried the groceries home, making a light dinner before opening the balcony doors, sitting in his chair, opening his book, and settling in to read.

The fading light forced Jonathon to close his book, and he checked the time before carrying his things inside and closing the balcony door. Foregoing his usual evening snack, he got cleaned up and decided he'd go to bed early, figuring that things might be better in the morning. He was about to climb the stairs when he heard a soft knock. Huffing softly, he walked downstairs, pulling open the door. Fabian stood on his doorstep, his expression unreadable. "I called the police and the emergency services. They wouldn't tell me much, but they did say which hospital he was taken to. It's not much, considering we don't know his name, but I'll take you in the morning if you want."

"You didn't have to do that."

"Yes, I did. I saw your face, and I knew I had hurt you. I did not mean that." Fabian took a small step closer. "Yesterday I said you had a gentle heart, and I meant it, you do. I should know that it would not allow you to turn away. I should not have acted as a Dummkopf." Fabian looked at his feet. "I should be more understanding and less like Oma."

"Well, thank you. I know it's hard for you to understand why I want to do this, but I need to know if he'll be okay." Jonathon tried to explain as best he could.

Fabian shook his head. "You are hoping you can help him. Maybe do for him what your Father Joda tried to do for you." His hand touched Jonathon's shoulder, fingers lightly massaging the muscle. "I don't know if you can, but I think I understand your need to try."

"Do you want to come in?" Jonathon asked, stepping back.

"Yes, very much, but I won't."

"Oh." Jonathon didn't understand that at all.

Fabian stepped just inside the door. "I find you very attractive." Jonathon felt Fabian's hand on his cheek, stroking softly. "If I come in, I will not be able to not touch you. So I will say good night, Gentle Heart, but I will come get you in the morning." Fabian brought their lips together in a scorching kiss that had Jonathon forgetting his own name and gasping for breath. Then Fabian backed away and disappeared into the night.

JONATHON woke in the morning, wishing for sun to dispel his dreams, but he got only clouds and drizzle. To say he hadn't slept well was an understatement. Whenever he'd closed his eyes, his dreams became a muddled mess of Fabian and Greg, with him lying in an alley, gasping for breath, reaching to one and then the other but never getting any help. More than once he'd awakened gasping for air, patting his body to make sure he was okay.

Throwing back the covers in a dramatic whoosh, he got out of bed, trying to will away the unsettled feeling that remained from the night. It wasn't working. His mind felt like it was floating, detached, and he walked downstairs, turning on the television before lying on the sofa. Almost instantly, he fell back to sleep.

"Johnny," he heard someone say his childhood nickname, not sure if he was awake or asleep. A hand brushed over his forehead, and he leaned into the touch, opening his eyes, seeing a pair of deep-brown ones shining back at him. "I knocked, but you didn't answer, but I could hear the television. Are you well?" Fabian asked, his voice soft and caring. "You were talking in your sleep." Jonathon tried to sit up, but Fabian touched his shoulder, and he relaxed back on the sofa. "I like you like this." He felt Fabian nuzzle his neck. "You look very good."

Jonathon remembered that he'd only been wearing his boxers when he'd moved to the sofa, and that became crystal clear as he felt a warm hand stroke his stomach and chest, lips touching his. "I should definitely get up." Part of him already was, but it had been so long since he'd been touched, and Fabian's hands felt so good, he lay back and closed his eyes, letting the sensations of warmth carry him for a while.

When the hands disappeared, he opened his eyes and saw Fabian standing next to him. "You make me want you very much."

Jonathon reached around Fabian's neck, pulling him down into a kiss. For most of the night, he'd been trying to figure out why he'd been holding back with Fabian, and he could never give himself an answer. But now he realized he didn't want to hold back any longer. Denying himself the affection and attention of someone he liked wasn't doing either of them any good. "I want you too," Jonathon gasped between kisses, his hand slinking beneath Fabian's shirt.

"Good." Fabian pulled away slowly. "I want this, but not here on the sofa. With you, we need to make love on a bed, not play around in the living room." Fabian seemed to be searching for his words, and Jonathon beamed for a second, because he'd found the perfect ones. But then he couldn't help wondering if it was just an accident. He wanted to believe Fabian knew what he'd said and meant the words, but he couldn't be sure.

Sitting up, he found himself kissed hard again before the lips backed away and Fabian helped him to his feet. "I'll go get dressed."

"Please do. Those don't leave much to the mind." Fabian smirked as Jonathon looked down, his boxers tented.

Rolling his eyes, Jonathon beat a hasty retreat up the stairs. "I'll just be a few minutes." Going to the wardrobe, he pulled on a pair of slacks and a shirt before finishing getting dressed. Once he was reasonably presentable, he went back downstairs, using the bathroom to finish getting ready.

"Mutti let me use the car; it'll be faster and more convenient than the subway," Fabian explained as he led the way toward the gumball machine Hans had used to pick him up at the airport.

"If this is your mother's car, whose car is that?"

"Opa's. He died a few years ago, and Oma uses it sometimes. Mostly it sits." Fabian opened the overhead door before getting behind the wheel, while Jonathon got into the passenger seat.

"I hope you drive better than Hans," Jonathon teased as Fabian started the engine, backing out of the courtyard; Jonathon got out, closing the door as the rain picked up. After he had hurried back inside the car, Fabian pulled away. "Good God," Jonathon exclaimed as Fabian barreled through a traffic signal. "You drive just like your brother." Holding onto anything available, he thought about praying as Fabian whipped through traffic, laying on the horn if anyone or anything got in their way. Finally, after seeing his life pass in front of his eyes—twice—they pulled into the hospital, parking in the parking structure before walking in the main entrance.

A severe-looking woman sat behind a desk, and Fabian walked up to her. Jonathon couldn't understand a word, but her body language was undeniable. Fabian could ask, cajole, even beg, but she was going to be about as helpful as a porcupine in a condom factory. Turning away, Fabian walked back toward him. "She would tell me nothing.

We can try the emergency entrance. He must have come through there, and maybe they can help us."

"I guess." Jonathon followed him through the corridors, following what he hoped were the right signs. "I shouldn't have sent you on this wild goose chase."

"What does that mean?"

"Sorry, it means we're looking for something we won't ever find," Jonathon explained as a set of doors opened in front of them and they stepped into a waiting room. Once again, Fabian walked up to the desk and began speaking to the woman sitting behind it. This time, at least, he didn't seem to run into a wall of resistance. Once again, Jonathon couldn't understand a word, but after a while, he saw Fabian point toward him before turning back to the woman. He saw her beginning to type, and then she began talking to Fabian rather animatedly, pointing toward a set of doors. Fabian thanked her—that part Jonathon understood—and then walked back over to where he waited.

"She said that they were hoping someone would call about him. She was on duty when he was brought in. They don't know his name, but she gave me directions to his floor."

"So he's alive?" Jonathon felt relieved.

"Yes. She said that he's"—Fabian thought a minute—"in critical condition," he proceeded slowly. "Got that from your television shows... and he's not doing well."

Fabian led them through the corridors to the elevator, and they rose, then stepped out into a world of dim lights and blinking machines and monitors. Fabian approached the desk and spoke to a woman whom Jonathon assumed was a nurse. She looked in her records and pointed toward one of the rooms.

"She said that only family can see him. I told her you were the one who saved his life, and she said she'd take us back to see him," Fabian explained, and Jonathon felt relief wash through him. At least he would get to see that he was being taken care of.

The nurse approached, and Jonathon thanked her in his best German. She smiled at him. "You are welcome," she replied before leading them down the corridor. "He hasn't woken up at all," she explained in superior English, "and we aren't sure he ever will." She pulled back a curtain, and Jonathon saw the small figure lying on the bed, tubes connected and instruments blinking.

Jonathon stared at the form on the bed. The boy's lip was swollen, and one eye was black and blue. He could only imagine what the rest of him looked like.

"Jonathon, it's okay," Fabian said.

"No, it's not." Jonathon swallowed hard. "This is someone's little boy. He may have been what you call a Strichjunge, a rent boy, but he was someone's son, and somewhere, someplace, someone loved him." Stepping forward, Jonathon walked to the bed, taking the small, almost feminine hand. "I'm sorry I couldn't do more to help you." Jonathon turned to the nurse. "Is there any chance you'll find out who he is?"

"We took blood, and the police are trying to identify him," she answered. "I have to return to my duties. Stay as long as you like. Having visitors might help him." She walked away, and Jonathon looked down at the perfect stranger with whom he had so much in common. He didn't know much about him, and yet he felt as though he knew everything—at least everything that was important.

Letting go of the young man's hand, Jonathon turned back to Fabian. "We can go." Turning to leave, Jonathon took a last look before following Fabian back to the desk. "Ma'am, would you call me if he wakes up?"

"I'll add it to his chart."

He gave her his mobile number and thanked her before following Fabian out of the hospital and back to the car. "Thank you." Jonathon got in the car when Fabian unlocked the door. "I know you thought this a fool's errand, but I needed to see him."

Fabian got in the car and leaned close to him. "I know you did, and I think I understand now. He was you, wasn't he? In a lot of ways, he is what you once were."

"Yes, exactly." Jonathon sighed softly, and he felt Fabian's hand glide around the back of his neck, tugging him gently into a kiss that went on and on.

"I was wrong, you don't have a gentle heart—you have a gentle soul." Fabian settled back into his seat. "Let's go home." Jonathon nodded his answer, and Fabian exited the parking garage, driving surprisingly sedately back to the house, parking the car in the courtyard and closing the door.

Jonathon got out of the car and walked around to his door, unlocking the apartment. Leaving the door open, he walked to the cupboard and took out the bottle of brandy, pouring two glasses, handing one to Fabian, who had followed him inside. Jonathon downed his glass and watched as Fabian did the same. Then he stepped forward, tugging Fabian into a hard, almost biting kiss. Without breaking the kiss, Jonathon tugged at the hem of Fabian's shirt, only letting the kiss slip away so he could pull it over Fabian's head. Then he was kissing him again, hands roaming over deep, rich, warm skin, thick chest hair sliding between his fingers.

Breathing hard, Jonathon tugged on Fabian's lower lip with his teeth until it popped back. Then, taking Fabian's hand, he led him up both flights of stairs to the bedroom.

"Is this what you want, Jonathon?" Fabian's question was answered when Jonathon tugged off his own shirt before pressing Fabian back onto the bed. Climbing on top of him, Jonathon kissed him hard. He felt Fabian's hands stroke down his back, holding tight as lips and tongues explored.

Jonathon let his own hands wander, sliding over hot skin, chest hair rough on his palms, Fabian grunting softly when he tugged at a nipple. He knew what he wanted, and he desperately wanted Fabian. Releasing the man's mouth, Jonathon ducked his head, sucking a tight, nubby nipple between his lips, running his teeth lightly over the skin. Fabian groaned loudly, arching his back as Jonathon ran his fingers up Fabian's throat and around his chin, slipping two fingers into his greedy mouth, where Fabian sucked hard.

Switching to the other bud, Jonathon bit down, listening to Fabian's moans and deep groans before lifting his head, looking Fabian in the eye. "You like that?"

"Yes. I like you, and I will take what you are willing to give," Fabian answered, his voice deep, eyes darkening rapidly. "I usually like things slow and gentle, but I can take hard and rough. I won't break."

Jonathon stopped. "I don't want to do anything you don't like."

Fabian cut off further words with a driving kiss that sent electricity running through Jonathon's brain. Grabbing Fabian's hands, Jonathon held them tight, extending their arms over Fabian's head, kissing him hard, teeth nipping slightly. Holding Fabian's wrists with one hand, Jonathon shifted on the bed, kneeling next to Fabian, devouring his rich skin with his eyes. This was one of the hottest men he'd ever laid eyes on, and Jonathon could barely believe he was in his bed. But beyond that, he had feelings for this man. What they were, he wasn't sure yet, because he refused to let himself define them. He just wasn't ready to go that far yet.

Using his free hand, he caressed Fabian's chest, tweaking each nipple slightly as his hand passed over each hard bud, with Fabian squirming and arching into the touch, making the most thrilling, moany groans deep in his throat, so rumbly that Jonathon could feel them through his palms. Leaning forward, Jonathon sucked on a nipple, tugging lightly as he ran his hand down Fabian's quivering stomach, following the trail lower. Deft fingers opened Fabian's belt, unfastening the pants before parting the fabric and skimming the burgeoning erection straining through thin fabric. "Johnny," Fabian gasped as he pushed the fabric aside, arching his back off the mattress as Jonathon grasped him. "Bitte, Johnny, bitte," was all he understood as a steady stream of pleading German flowed out of Fabian.

"You look so beautiful, all stretched out for me," Jonathon cooed as he stroked lightly, the German becoming more frantic, Fabian's hips doing their best to push off the mattress. "I know what you want, and you'll get it, I promise, but not right now," Jonathon whispered as he ran his tongue along Fabian's side, the smooth skin rich and warm,

Fabian squirming to get away while at the same time Jonathon could feel his need to get closer.

Tightening his grip slightly, Jonathon kissed his way down Fabian's stomach before releasing Fabian's length, replacing his hand with his lips, letting his hand slip away from Fabian's wrists. Kissing his way down the throbbing cock as the stream of German increased. Fingers carded through his hair, hips pumping, cock sliding against his lips. Fabian's moans became more frantic, and Jonathon pulled back, bringing their lips together in a bruising kiss that left them both panting.

Jonathon suddenly found himself tugged onto his back, pressed against the mattress as Fabian went wild, kissing hard, their bodies undulating together as Fabian kicked his legs, and Jonathon heard a thud as Fabian's pants hit the floor.

Fingers worked open his belt, and a hand thrust his pants down before Fabian jumped off the bed, tugging the pants ferociously off his legs. "Want you naked, Johnny," Fabian growled richly before kissing him again, their bodies melding together, cocks sliding, chests mashing together, their mouths pleading silently with one another.

"Fuck, Fabian," Jonathon gasped as his mind took flight, skin hypersensitive to every touch, every movement as he felt Fabian's hands slip beneath him, palms cupping his butt, fingers gripping as Fabian's cries reached a fever pitch. Eyes clamped shut, body rigidly throbbing, Jonathon felt Fabian's searing release on his skin, and with a gasp, Fabian collapsed on top of him, breathing like a marathoner against his neck.

"You nearly killed me," Fabian gasped between breaths, and Jonathon felt light kisses on his shoulder. "I make you happy as soon as I can breathe."

Jonathon could wait, and he stroked Fabian's skin, immensely pleased that he could give the younger man such rapturous pleasure. Rolling them over, he pressed Fabian into the mattress, kissing and stroking until he felt Fabian's legs around his waist. "Want you, Johnny," Fabian breathed into his ear, and Jonathon stroked his hands down strong thighs, teasing them along his cleft before ghosting the very tips over Fabian's opening.

"I need to get some things," Jonathon whispered, and after a soft kiss, he lifted himself off Fabian and hurried to the bathroom. The steps had never passed under his feet so fast, and in what felt like the blink of an eye, he was back, taking in every inch of warm skin.

Tossing the bottle of lube on the bed, he set the rest of the supplies on the nightstand before climbing back on the bed, kissing Fabian again. "How do you like it?"

Fabian's legs wrapped back around his waist and his arms slipped around his neck—Jonathon had his answer. Finding the bottle, he slicked his fingers, teasing and swirling them around Fabian's opening before slowly pressing one inside. Tight heat gripped him, and he sank his finger deeper, wondering how long it had been for Fabian. Somehow, he'd assumed that Fabian could have anyone he wanted and probably had, but his body told him a very different story, especially when he curled his finger and the surprised gasp he received told him that Fabian wasn't as experienced as he'd assumed. Easily finding the magic spot, Jonathon smiled against Fabian's lips as the German moans began again.

Carefully adding a second finger, he used those incredible sounds to gauge Fabian's reaction. When the sounds tapered off, he shifted tactics, and when they picked up, he repeated what he was doing, and when he went operatic soprano, he knew he'd hit the jackpot. Sliding his fingers away, he reached to the nightstand for the condom, watching Fabian's eyes as he prepared himself. "Is this okay?"

Fabian nodded, and Jonathon pressed forward as slowly as his body would let him. He saw Fabian's eyes widen and heard him gasp, and only when he felt Fabian push against him did he move again. "Please, Johnny, don't stop."

"Don't want to hurt you," he responded as he nipped Fabian's neck. "Would never want to hurt you," he added as his hips met Fabian's butt, and he held still, the wet heat around him gripping tight, and he wondered if this was Fabian's first time. Silently chiding himself for not asking, he got lost in his self-recrimination until Fabian grabbed his butt, pressing them closer together.

Slowly, Jonathon began to move, withdrawing and then pressing back inside. A loud gasp melded into a deep, rich groan. "Don't stop, Johnny."

He had no intention of stopping as he locked his eyes onto Fabian's, feeling their bodies move together as his own desire built and he found himself moaning deeply. "Fuck, Fabian!" His head throbbed and he felt his heart open as those deep-brown eyes looked back at him, pleading with him, imploring him.

Stroking along Fabian's length, Jonathon gasped as Fabian grabbed the headboard, body stretched out, Fabian's pleasure in his hands. The trust he was being given drove him higher, and Jonathon gasped as his mind and body reacted at the same time, surging forward to claim this wonderful man.

"Johnny, gonna…." The rest of Fabian's thought came out in a garble of German and English, but Jonathon didn't have to understand the words to know how Fabian felt—he could barely form a coherent thought as his passion overrode everything, and as his climax built, he felt Fabian reach the precipice along with him. With dual cries that carried out of the open windows, they plummeted together.

Barely able to breathe, head spinning, Jonathon tried his best not to just flop on top of Fabian, so he stayed where he was, breathing heavily, looking down at the thoroughly debauched younger man. Slowly, their bodies separated, both of them wincing at the loss. Fabian reached for his hand, taking it and tugging him forward, and Jonathon rested next to the younger man, each holding the other in a way Jonathon hadn't thought he'd ever be held again. And the kisses, soft and warm, gentle and kind… dare he think, loving? It was almost too much for Jonathon to hope for, but that was how they felt, and that was what remained at the forefront of Jonathon's mind as his eyes closed and he drifted off into dreams now filled with waltzes.

CHAPTER Seven

JONATHON woke to an empty bed, not that there was anything unusual in that. He'd awakened to an empty bed for years now, but somehow he still checked, just like he had the afternoon he and Fabian….

Jonathon stopped the thought in its tracks. He and Fabian had, hell, he didn't know what to call it—fucked, he guessed. At the time he'd thought they might be making love, but boy, had he been wrong, and that became readily apparent when he'd woken from his short nap to an empty bed and an empty apartment. What was worse, Fabian hadn't returned at all that day and hadn't for almost a week. The following day, Saturday, he'd said good-bye to Jeana, not letting on about his disappointment, seeing her to the train and waving good-bye. He kept wondering what could be wrong and had even worried. He resolved to give him the day—after all, they weren't joined at the hip, and Fabian did have a life of his own—but on Sunday he saw Fabian leaving the house, hurrying down the sidewalk. He knew Fabian saw him too, but he didn't even wave or acknowledge him in any way, and that really hurt. He'd wallowed in that hurt until Tuesday, when it morphed into anger. He spent two days going over what he could have done wrong, and he determined that the wallowing would, somehow, end.

By Thursday when he woke, he'd given up and figured Fabian had gotten what he wanted and had moved on. What could he do? He'd made a fool of himself over a handsome younger guy, and that was that. Getting out of bed, Jonathon pulled on sweatpants and walked to the kitchen to make coffee. Once the pot was ready, he poured a cup and made his way to the balcony, grabbing the book he was reading, reminding himself to make another stop at the bookstore. The stack of books he'd already read was growing by the day. Sitting in his chair, he opened the book and disappeared into the action-adventure story.

The ringing phone pulled him out of the story, and he picked it up, checking the number on the display. Not recognizing it, he almost let it go to voice mail. "Hello?" he said tentatively, expecting a wrong number.

"Herr Pfister?" a woman's voice said, pronouncing the P ever so slightly. "I'm Greta Nobelkopf, we met at Vienna General Hospital a few days ago."

"You're the nurse who helped us, I remember you." Jonathon thought of the boy in the hospital bed. "Is he awake?"

"I'm sorry." He could hear the sadness in her voice. "The doctors have determined that he will never wake and have authorized that we turn off all machines. You were the only one who visited him." He heard her swallow. "I could be fired for this," her voice softened to a whisper, "but I called because no one should die alone."

Jonathon didn't give it a second thought. "I'll be there as fast as I can." He heard her thank him and then disconnect. Jonathon jumped up, throwing the book on the table as he rushed upstairs. Stripping off his sweats, he pulled on some clothes, grabbed his things, remembering the subway map he'd purchased a few days earlier, and hurried out the door to the nearest subway station.

It took him a while and at least one missed train—which left him cursing under his breath and hoping he wasn't too late—before he found himself walking into the hospital emergency exit, retracing his steps through the hospital until he made it to the floor he remembered and saw Greta, who hurried to him. "You are just in time," she said softly and led him back to the room he remembered.

A doctor stood near the bed, and Jonathon waited while Greta stepped to him and they talked in low tones before the doctor motioned him over. "I understand you were the one who tried to help him."

"Yes. Do you know his name?" The doctor consulted the chart, shaking his head, and Jonathon looked to Greta. "No one should die without a name either," he said, and she nodded. "So we'll call you Johan," Jonathon added as he looked at the boyish face, now even paler than before, and saw the small chest barely rise and fall. Moving closer, he lifted the hand that didn't have IVs attached and entwined their fingers.

Jonathon heard movement in the room but didn't look up from the boy's face as he heard the monitor that called out his heartbeat slow and quiet. Unlike the movies, in this case there was no long tone, only quiet as the chest stopped moving and a young man's life ended. Jonathon held the hand awhile longer, tears running down his cheeks for Johan and Greg both.

Slowly, he set the hand down onto the bed, releasing the fingers before sliding his hand away. Stepping away from the bed, he looked up at the doctor and Greta before walking toward the door and out into the hall. Searching his pockets, he found a tissue and wiped his eyes, thinking. He'd held onto so much pain and grief for so long. It was definitely time to let go.

Greta stepped from the room, and Jonathon thanked her before heading toward the elevator and out of the hospital, back into the sunshine. Instead of walking to the subway, he found himself strolling along the Ringstrasse, walking aimlessly. Finding himself outside a café, he stepped inside to find computers instead of coffee. Sitting down, he paid for a few minutes and, without thinking, punched in the name of his school. Getting the phone number, he jotted it down and left the building, fishing his phone out of his pocket and dialing before he lost his nerve.

"Good morning, St. Lawrence School for Boys."

"Yes, good morning." He tried to think how to proceed. "I was wondering if Father Joda is still there?" Not very likely, he chastised himself softly. It had been almost thirty years.

"He's no longer the principal, but he's here most days. I can check to see if he's in the building. If I find him, can I tell him what this is regarding?" she inquired very professionally.

"I'm a former student, and I wanted to speak with him. I'm calling from Vienna, Austria."

"I'll see if I can find him. Just a minute." He heard her set the phone down, and he pictured the office in his mind. It probably looked almost the same, with its dark wood and the statue of St. Lawrence holding the cross standing next to the statue of Mary with her white veil. Heck, the phone was probably the same dial phone in avocado green.

After a few minutes, he heard shuffling, and then someone picked up the phone. "Hello," a male voice said, very loudly, and he heard a voice in the background. "Father Joda, put in your hearing aid." More fumbling followed, and then he heard another "Hello," this time at a more normal volume.

"Father Joda?" Jonathon asked, almost chickening out and hanging up. "This is Jonathon Pfister, I was one of your students many years ago."

Silence greeted him, and for a second he wondered if the line was dead. "Jonathon, is that you?"

"Yes, Father Joda—you do remember."

"Of course I remember you. How could I forget?" Jonathon heard shifting on the other end of the line. "I have to sit," he explained. The line went quiet, and then he heard Father Joda's voice again. "I could never forget you, Jonathon. You were my one disappointment."

"Oh." Jonathon felt his defenses rise, and he wondered why he'd even called at all and what he was expecting. "Well, you—"

"Johnny." Father Joda used the nickname he'd gone by in school. "*I* was the disappointment, not you." He heard the old man's voice crack, regret plain. "I should have believed you and had faith in you. I let your past dictate my beliefs, and I have always regretted it. I know now that not only you but other boys were abused, and I had the chance to stop it, but I didn't."

Jonathon began pacing the sidewalk, walking back and forth in front of the café, having no idea what to say. Then he stopped and looked across the way at the neo-Gothic church with its huge stone spires pointing to the sky. "I forgive you." He almost immediately felt a lightness creep into his spirit. "And I thank you for helping me. I know you didn't believe me then, but you still helped me, and for that I'm grateful."

"Thank you. You've been in my thoughts many times. Sheila told me you're in Vienna, do you live there?"

"No, I'm visiting for a while, but I live on Long Island and teach third grade. I became a teacher because I didn't want what happened to me to happen to anyone else." Jonathon heard a beeping through his phone and realized his battery was running low. "Father Joda, I have to go, my battery is about to run out."

"Will you come see me when you get back?" He heard excitement in the man's voice. "I'd really like to see you."

"I'll do that." Jonathon said good-bye and closed the phone, smiling for the first time in days. Walking back toward the subway station, he stopped near the stairs, surprised at feeling lighter than he could remember since Greg's passing. Changing his mind, he began walking along the ring road toward the apartment, letting the sunshine warm him both inside and out.

It took a while, but a few hours later, he'd walked past the Austrian Parliament and the museums, as well as the Hofburg Palace, before reaching the opera house. He couldn't stop himself from thinking of the fun time he'd had at the opera with Fabian. Jonathon looked at the ornate building for a few minutes before turning away and forcing Fabian out of his mind. There were plenty of men in a city as large as Vienna, and he was going out to try to meet some of them.

Walking the last few blocks to the apartment, he turned the corner and stopped at the passageway. Lifting his head, he said a last good-bye to Johan, silently wishing him peace. Then he turned and made his way home.

OPENING the courtyard gate, Jonathon was surprised to find it empty. He walked across the space, remarking to himself on how nice it would be if it didn't have to hold the cars. Approaching his door, he took out his key and inserted it into the lock, only to find the door unlocked, which was not how he'd left it. Pushing open the door, he walked inside and saw Fabian sitting at the small table in his kitchen with what looked like the now nearly empty brandy bottle in front of him.

"What are you doing here?" Jonathon asked snappily, not in the mood for whatever lame excuses Fabian had on the tip of his tongue. He'd been played for the fool once; it wasn't going to happen again.

Fabian lifted his head, eyes clouded by what Jonathon figured was quite a bit of alcohol. "I came to say that I am sorry and to explain, but you were not here, and…." He hiccupped and made a sour face before swallowing.

"You decided that drinking would make you feel better," Jonathon finished and walked to the table, picking up the bottle before closing it and putting it away. "I've heard your apology, and I'm not really interested in your explanation or excuses. So I suggest you stand up, if you can, and go home." Jonathon pointed toward the door, and Fabian stood up as best he could before weaving his way toward Jonathon. Stumbling, Fabian reached out, and Jonathon caught him in his arms, steadying him as best he could while guiding Fabian toward the door.

Fabian kissed him. A sloppy, brandy-soaked kiss, before hugging him tight, resting his head on Jonathon's shoulders. "I am sorry, Johnny," he slurred. "Oma, she...."

Jonathon felt Fabian's weight against him and knew he wasn't going very far before he passed out. "Can you walk up the stairs if I help you?"

"We go to your bedroom?" Fabian asked, and he started toward the stairs, with Jonathon helping him. Somehow, they managed to make it to the living room level, and Jonathon got Fabian to the bathroom, where he collapsed onto the floor. Just what he needed—a sloppy drunk. After Fabian threw up a few times, Jonathon helped him up and onto the sofa, where Fabian flopped onto the cushions and was soon snoring. He knew he should let someone know where Fabian was, but Hans should be in school, and with both cars gone, he figured neither Hanna nor Oma were home, so he decided to let Fabian sleep it off. Covering him with a blanket, Jonathon picked up his book and opened the balcony doors before settling down to read.

The quiet afternoon left Jonathon with plenty of time to think, and a number of times he found himself staring at Fabian, watching him sleep. He kept telling himself it was only because he was concerned about him, but after a while, he wasn't buying it anymore. There was something about Fabian that fascinated him, but he couldn't put his finger on it. From what he'd said, or more accurately, slurred, Oma had done something, and Fabian had stayed away because of it.

Turning away from the sleeping man, he thought about everything that had happened, and he couldn't figure out how one day could possibly have turned everything in his life on its head, but today had been one of those days. Looking back, similar days in his life came to mind: his parents' death, a day that resulted in him living on the street. The day he met Father Joda and thought he might have found a place in the world where he could belong, only to have that place yanked away when his trust had been betrayed by the man he'd thought of as his savior. The biggest and best day of his life, when he'd met Greg at a school parents' night that had kicked off the happiest seventeen years of his life. The day Greg died, when he thought his life was over. And today, when the death of a young man—whose life, so very much like his own could have been—had ushered in forgiveness and, dare he think, healing.

Fabian rolling in his sleep pulled Jonathon's attention away from his ruminations to the man slumbering on his sofa. He watched as the blanket fell to the floor, Fabian's arms flopping above his head and pulling his shirt up just enough to expose a few inches of dark, rich skin around his middle. The man was beautiful, there was no doubt about it, but Jonathon knew almost nothing about him. They'd had a few dates and danced together. Sure, they'd talked some, but maybe they needed to really talk before....

"Before nothing," he said to himself as he got up from his chair, reminding himself that the man had dumped him as soon as he'd gotten what he wanted. But damn, it was hard staying mad at a man who looked so adorable when he slept. Jonathon forced himself to turn away before walking down the stairs to make himself dinner.

"WHAT happened to me?" Jonathon heard Fabian's voice from behind him. Turning around, he saw the younger man holding his head, lowering himself into a chair. "My head feels like it is a balloon."

Jonathon took pity on him, opening the refrigerator and pulling out a bottle of apple juice and pouring a glass. "The sugar and sweetness will help," Jonathon said as he thunked the glass on the table, hearing Fabian's soft groan. "Don't expect any sympathy from me when it comes to a hangover," Jonathon added a little loudly, and Fabian took a sip of the juice, setting the glass gingerly on the table.

"I guess not," Fabian answered, looking at him with big puppy-dog eyes.

"Do you want to tell me why you were drinking in my kitchen?" Jonathon turned back to his cooking, adding egg to the potatoes in the pan, along with salt and pepper.

"I was looking for you," Fabian answered, and Jonathon smiled a little when he saw Fabian wince at the sound of his own voice. "I wanted to try to explain why I am behaving like such a donkey."

"You mean like an ass," Jonathon corrected. "Because you were—behaving like an ass, that is." He turned back to his pan, lowering the heat so the eggs could cook without burning. "Not that I should even listen to you after what you did." Jonathon thought he should just send Fabian on his way now that he was awake and obviously able to walk on his own. Turning off the heat, Jonathon got a plate down from the cupboard and placed the fritatta on it before setting his meal on the table. He saw Fabian look at the food and turn a slight shade of green. "It's not for you, so just sip your juice." Jonathon took his seat. "If you want to explain, then you have until I finish my dinner, because after that I'm going out for the evening." Jonathon took his first bite.

"Oma came looking for me," Fabian started, his speech slow and measured. "I heard her in the courtyard after we made love. You were asleep, and I did not want to wake you, so I got up and dressed before she could knock on the door."

"So? She's your grandmother. She's not your wife or something."

"Oma's old-fashioned, and she said if she caught me again, she would throw me out of the house. So I dressed and left, figuring I'd come back after she was gone. But that woman sees everything, and she dragged me back to the house."

"Fabian." Jonathon raised his hand to stop him. "You're thirty years old. I've met a few mama's boys in my time, but you're the first grandma's boy I've ever met. If you aren't man enough to stand up to her and tell her how you feel and what you want, I don't need you in my life."

Fabian took another sip of the apple juice before pushing the glass away. "I did tell her, this morning." Fabian lowered his head to the table, and Jonathon had to stop himself from reaching out to stroke it. "She left afterwards, saying she was going to church to pray for my soul."

Jonathon shook his head slowly before taking another bite. "Fabian, your grandmother can't guilt you into changing who you are. You're a gay man."

Fabian lifted his head, holding it in his hands. "She also said that if I didn't behave properly, I could find another place to live, so I was wondering if I could live here with you." Fabian's eyes had the expectant look of a dog that was about to receive big, juicy bone.

"No," Jonathon answered softly, and he saw Fabian's hope deflate. "You can't run from this."

"I'm not running. She's kicking me out."

"Yes, you are. Your mother supports you, and your brother idolizes you. Think about it—if you move in here, you're just transferring the problem to a different location." Jonathon reached out, talking Fabian's hand. "When she first caught you and kicked you out, you ran and stayed away for eighteen months. In that time, did she change her attitude? Did you help her understand how you feel? No. All that happened was that you were away from the brother and mother who love you. And when you came back, the same problem returned, because running doesn't settle anything." A car door closing outside made both their heads turn, and Fabian stood up, steadying himself on the table.

"You're right," Fabian said as he took his first step toward the door.

"Fabian," Jonathon called softly. "Why did you come to find me in the first place?"

"It doesn't matter now." Fabian took a few unsteady steps toward the door. "I came because I missed you, and because"—he sighed loudly—"I think I love you."

Jonathon felt the air whoosh from his lungs. That had been the last thing he'd expected to hear, and he felt his mouth hang open in complete surprise. Standing up, Jonathon walked to Fabian, putting his arms around him. He didn't know what it was he felt for Fabian at that moment, but that admission was a big step for anyone.

"And maybe it's time I stood up for who I love. I didn't before, but this time I will." Standing taller and definitely more steadily on his feet, Fabian slipped out of his arms and walked toward the door, closing it behind him, and Jonathon watched through the window as Fabian walked around his grandmother's car toward the house.

Almost as soon as Fabian had left, Jonathon began pacing around the kitchen. He'd done a lot of talking and had given Fabian a lot of cheap advice, and he started to wonder if he'd done the right thing. "Shit," Jonathon murmured as he ran his fingers through his hair. What if he'd messed up Fabian's relationship with his family? It wasn't as though Jonathon actually *had* a family like Fabian's. What the hell did he know about things like that in the first place? What if Fabian did what Jonathon said he should and it messed everything up for him? Jonathon slumped into one of the chairs, wondering why he hadn't just kept his big mouth shut.

Fabian had come into the apartment to tell him, Jonathon Pfister, that he loved him. Jonathon swallowed hard. Fabian loved him. That warm, tingly feeling he thought he'd never feel again started at the base of his spine and spread upward, growing into a wealth of fire and shivers of delight as it reached his neck, before blooming into a glow he'd only felt one other time in his life. Was it too early? Probably, but that hadn't stopped him with Greg, and look what had happened. He'd had seventeen marvelous years with Greg. That didn't mean he'd have the same thing with Fabian, but those simple words from Fabian helped Jonathon feel alive, really alive, for the first time in a long time. God, all Jonathon could think was: what if Fabian suddenly realized that Jonathon wasn't worth it?

Jonathon jumped as he heard a knock on his door and looked up from where he'd been staring during his worried ruminations. Hans peered in the window, looking worried as only a teenager could. Jonathon motioned for Hans to come in, and the door opened. "What's going on?" He tried to keep his concerns out of his voice.

"Oma and Fabian are"—he swallowed—"talking loudly, and I was wondering if I could study here for a while. I have a big exam on Monday." Jonathon could tell by the way he bit his lip that Hans was treading delicately around what was probably a full-blown fight between Fabian and his grandmother.

"Are they fighting?"

Hans nodded a few times. "I know that Fabian likes men, and that's okay, I guess. But why do he and Oma have to yell all the time?"

Jonathon motioned Hans toward the other chair. "Would you like something to drink?"

"Can you make Apfelschorle? Its apple juice and some mineral water," Hans went on to explain as he spread out his books on the table. Jonathon poured the juice and added some sparkling water to the glass before placing it on the table, and since it looked good, he made himself one as well.

"Your Oma and Fabian," Jonathon started to explain as he pulled out the chair across from Hans, "have very different views on the way Fabian should live his life."

"I know. Oma wants him to get married and have babies. She even invited one of her friend's granddaughters over for dinner last night. She was pretty." Hans smiled and colored a little. "But it only made Fabian angry, and he didn't talk to her very much." Hans took a drink from his glass. "Oma likes things the old-fashioned way, and I do as well, sometimes." Hans turned his attention to his books, but Jonathon could tell he wasn't really paying attention to them. "Will they ever stop fighting?"

"Maybe," Jonathon answered. "I don't know your Oma very well, but she loves you and Fabian very much, just like your mother does. And she ultimately wants him to be happy. Right now she thinks she knows best regarding what will make him happy. Fabian needs to show her as well as tell her that he knows what is best for him, and sometimes those talks aren't easy and involve yelling."

"Oh." Hans went back to his books, and Jonathon got back up, going to the sink to clean up his dishes. Running the water, he handwashed the few dishes before letting them dry in the dish drainer.

"I am not bothering you?"

"No, Hans," Jonathon answered as he wiped his hands. "I'm going to go upstairs and sit. You can stay here if you like or come up." Hans closed his books and picked both them and his glass up from the table and followed Jonathon up the stairs. "What are you studying?" Jonathon asked as he sat on the sofa, picking his book up from the coffee table.

Hans showed him the book cover, but it meant nothing to him, since the title was in German. "Art history. It's one of my favorite subjects."

"And necessary if you want to be an art restorer."

Hans nodded his agreement and returned his attention to his studies, while Jonathon opened his book and began to read with part of his attention tuned to the pages and part listening for Fabian's footsteps outside.

Voices drifted through the walls, not loud enough to actually understand, but enough to know that something was definitely going on. Jonathon looked to Hans and saw him lift his head from his studies, biting his lower lip. Then the sound stopped and Jonathon found himself straining to hear, but there was nothing. Returning his attention to his book, Jonathon tried to concentrate but felt his earlier worries return.

The sound of the lift door and the crunch of tires told him that Hanna was home. He heard the car engine stop and footsteps on the gravel and finally the muffled sound of a door closing, then more voices, slightly louder, both most definitely female. "Come on." Jonathon set down his book. "Let's get out of here."

Hans followed him down the stairs. "Where are we going?"

"The pastry shop around the corner is still open. Let's get a bite and some coffee." The wondering was getting to him, and Jonathon could tell it was affecting Hans even more. Grabbing his keys and wallet from the counter, Jonathon held the door for Hans before following him through the courtyard and out the gate.

Accompanied by a Waltz

They hurried down the sidewalk and had almost reached the corner when Hans stopped and turned around. "It's Fabian."

Jonathon waited, and Fabian hurriedly caught up with them. "Where are you going?" Fabian asked between breaths.

"To the coffee shop," Hans answered. "We could hear you and Oma yelling through the walls, and then Mutti got home." Hans let the implications hang in the air.

"I know." Fabian ruffled his younger brother's hair, and Hans squirmed away with a laugh. "I took your advice," Fabian told Jonathon, "as you and half the neighborhood heard." They continued walking, turning the corner. "It didn't go well at first, but then she started to listen, at least to some things. When Mutti got home, the two of them went at it like cats and dogs. I've never seen Mutti so angry."

"Not even the time you dyed your hair blue in the bathtub?" Hans chided with a wicked smile on his face.

Jonathon couldn't hold back the laughter when Fabian blushed like a schoolgirl. "That was a long time ago. And yes, today was worse."

Hans whistled as they reached the pastry shop, and Fabian held the doors open, touching Jonathon's hand as he passed. Jonathon gave Fabian a quick smile before standing next to Hans, looking over the pastry case in wonder. "Get whatever you like," Jonathon told Hans as the lady behind the counter spoke to him in German, and Jonathon turned to Fabian. "Order for me, please. I have no idea what anything is."

Fabian nodded and placed the orders, and Jonathon paid at the register. They sat at one of the few empty tables and waited. "Do you think Mutti and Oma will be okay?" Hans asked.

"They'll be fine," Fabian said with a wink at Jonathon. "Mutti is just letting Oma know that we're her children and that Oma cannot run all of our lives. Believe me, you will be happy for this day."

The server brought their pastries and coffee, efficiently setting them on the table and leaving. Jonathon brought the cup to his lips, testing the coffee as Hans turned to Fabian, his fork in his hand.

"You and Jonathon *bumsen?*"

Jonathon might not have known much German, but that word he knew, and he barely managed to set his cup back on the saucer before coughing and choking.

Thankfully, Fabian spoke up, looking at Jonathon for reassurance. "No, we are not, Hans. We...." Fabian sighed, and Jonathon let him stumble as he decided what to tell his brother. "I have feelings for Jonathon that are deeper than just sex." Jonathon watched as Fabian set down his cup and pushed his plate away. "I don't know what Jonathon and I are right now." The adorably pleading look on Fabian's face went right to Jonathon's heart. "But I do know it's more than *bumsen*, to use your word." Fabian grabbed his brother around the neck, applying his knuckles to the top of his head. "You shouldn't be using that word anyway."

"Hans," Jonathon broke in, figuring he'd give Fabian a break, "your brother and I are exploring a relationship," he explained, hoping he wasn't wrong. And when he saw the smile on Fabian's face, he knew he'd explained things correctly.

"But you are... aren't you?" Hans asked wickedly as he shoveled in a mouthful of his cake.

"That is none of your business," Jonathon answered levelly. "And you shouldn't ask such questions." He picked up his cup. "Would you like us asking about your virginity?" he added, taking a sip from his cup, winking at Fabian as Hans nearly choked to death.

They finished their cake and coffee without further drama and walked back to the house. Opening the gate, Jonathon found himself listening but hearing nothing. Hans walked toward the house. "Don't forget your books," Jonathon called, and Hans veered off, following them to the apartment, where he rushed upstairs, grabbing his books from the table before hurrying back down.

"Danke schön, Jonathon," Hans called as he reached the door.

"Before you go," Jonathon said as Hans reached for the door handle, "next Saturday, once you're done with school, I was wondering if you'd like to go to the Prater to celebrate the end of school and your graduation to university."

Hans's grin told him everything he needed to know. "Yes, thank you," Hans chimed as he hurried out the door, feet crunching on the gravel.

"You certainly made him happy," Fabian said as arms slipped around Jonathon's waist, and he felt Fabian's chest press against his back, the arms tightening, drawing them closer. "Did you really mean what you said? Do you really want a relationship?"

Jonathon turned around. "I have to be honest—I don't know what I want, but I definitely know what I don't." Jonathon looked toward the floor. "I know I'm not being very fair to you, but I need some time to work things through."

"I think I understand, and yes, I can be patient." Fabian softly kissed his neck. "But I meant what I said earlier."

"I know you did." Jonathon leaned closer, kissing Fabian oh-so-softly, feeling the warmth of Fabian's lips as he felt a hand slide into his.

"Come with me." Fabian led him up both sets of stairs to the bedroom. "You mean much more to me than just sex," Fabian said softly, "and I'll give you all the time you need, I promise. But right now there's something I'd like you to do for me." Fabian led him to the bed, lying down before pulling Jonathon next to him, arms holding him tight.

"So if you didn't bring me up here for *bumsen*"—Fabian chuckled lightly in his ear—"then what did you bring me here for?" Jonathon stroked his hand over the soft fabric covering Fabian's chest.

"I want you to tell me about your Greg," Fabian answered softly. "I know he was your first true love and that you were together for a long time, but I really want to know what he was like."

"Fabian." Jonathon felt his chest clench. "Do you know what you're asking?" he asked as Fabian shifted them on the bed so Jonathan was lying on his back with Fabian resting on his side, watching him with eyes as warm as hot chocolate.

"Yes. I'm asking you to give up a small piece of his memory." Fabian's eyes implored him, and Jonathon felt himself still as he tried to decide not if he should do what Fabian asked, but if he actually could.

"I'm not sure where to start," Jonathon answered softly as he stared up at Fabian. It felt weird to think about telling Fabian about Greg. He'd been trying his best not to compare Fabian to Greg, and in his mind, he'd sort of compartmentalized the two in some ways, keeping Greg's memories separate from the ones with Fabian.

"How did you meet?" Fabian smoothed his hand over Jonathon's cheek.

Jonathon closed his eyes, and he couldn't help smiling. "I'd been teaching a few years, and it was parents' night at the school. Once a year, they had an open house where parents could meet the teachers and see the classrooms. I was already teaching third grade, and Greg's oldest son had just started kindergarten. He had no reason to come to my classroom, but he wandered through, carrying the cutest little girl in his arms. Jeana was about two at the time." Jonathon stopped for a second, the memory so strong it threatened to overpower him, almost as fresh as if it had happened yesterday. Forcing his eyes open, he looked at Fabian, regrounding himself in the present. "He was tall and broad, a few years younger than I am now, but he didn't look it. I can remember just the first start of gray in his hair, which I remember wanting to reach out and touch. He was the most beautiful man I'd ever seen, and he remained that way until he died."

"Did you know he was gay?" Fabian asked softly, touching Jonathon's hair right above the ears.

"The minute I saw him, there was no doubt in my mind. But I didn't approach him other than to show him around the classroom and talk to him about the beautiful child he was carrying. The first time I saw him smile was when we talked about his children." Jonathon did his best to mimic that smile, and he felt Fabian kiss him softly as a reward for his efforts. "The second time was when he left my classroom and I said I hoped I'd see him again soon, and I did. About a week later, he stopped in at the school to make a donation to one of the never-ending fund drives and asked me to lunch. I had to turn him down because I couldn't leave school grounds, but then he asked me to dinner." Jonathon shifted on the bed, running his hand along the skin of Fabian's arm. "I couldn't believe he could ever be interested in me, but there was one thing about Greg—he knew what he wanted. I know Doreen was pregnant when she and Greg married, and I always wondered if she didn't engineer it somehow."

"How long were you together while he was married?"

"We weren't. We had dinner together almost every night and even kissed a few times." Jonathon smiled as he remembered the heady feeling of those first kisses, so filled with excitement and promise. "Greg filed for divorce shortly after we met, but we never got physical until the separation became legal and he'd moved out of the house." Jonathon had no intention of going into those details. "Doreen always blamed me for stealing her husband, but I never did. Of Greg's three children, only Jeana will have anything to do with me. Their mother spent much of her time over the years venting her venom about me and Greg to those kids, even though Greg did his best by those kids and her."

"It sounds as though Greg really loved you." Fabian's voice held the slightest hint of jealousy.

For the first time, Jonathon felt tears threaten, but he stopped himself and smiled instead. "He did." Jonathon smoothed a hand along Fabian's cheek, as though he were trying to caress away the unnecessary emotion. "Greg was always a very busy man, but he never forgot a birthday or anniversary, and he told me he loved me every single day. He was honorable, loving, and generous to a fault." Jonathon reached to the nightstand, picking up the photograph and handing it to Fabian. "For the longest time, I thought he was the only person who'd ever loved me." Jonathon touched the photograph with a finger. "But I'm coming to realize that I've been loved in more ways than I realized. Jeana, even when her mother tried to turn her against both Greg and me, still loved me and showed it."

"Of course you were loved. You said your parents were killed, but they must have loved you."

Jonathon nodded his head against the pillow. "And I found out today that Father Joda loved me as well." Jonathon went on to tell Fabian about the call from the hospital and how Johan's death had prompted him to call Father Joda, as well as the revelations that call had brought about.

"See," Fabian beamed. "Of course you were loved. I can't imagine anyone getting to know you and not loving you." Fabian leaned closer, capturing his mouth in a kiss that surprised Jonathon with its loving softness. Jonathon slipped his arms around Fabian's neck, deepening the kiss. "Do you ever imagine that it's Greg you're kissing instead of me?"

"No, I've never done that. When I'm with you, I know it's you," Jonathon said as he pulled Fabian back down on top of him, curling their legs together as he held Fabian close, losing himself in the kisses and touches as their desire quickly escalated from a slow simmer to a fast boil. Clothes disappeared and hands slid across warm skin, touching, caressing, lips kissing, tongues tasting. Soft gasps and murmurs of pleasure drifted on the breeze that blew in through the open windows, the night air fresh and cooling, caressing their skin as it followed the flow of warm, exploring hands. Jonathon arched into Fabian's hands, eyes clouding with desire as he heard soft music float on the breeze. Without thought, they moved to the accompaniment, their bodies flowing and hearts stirring, their lovemaking moving to the flowing melody of the waltz.

CHAPTER Eight

JONATHON woke to something that was starting to become very familiar, too familiar—Fabian pressed tight against him, arms encircling his waist, holding him tight, like Fabian wasn't going to let him go. They never started out this way, each of them preferring to fall asleep separately, but during the night, they both seemed to search the other out, curling close in the darkness. For over a week, Fabian had spent most nights in his bed, and while Jonathon knew he still had a month before he had to leave, he also already knew he was going to miss the man sleeping next to him. At first, he'd stupidly thought it was just the company and that his ardor for Fabian would lessen over time, but it hadn't. In less than a month, Jonathon had somehow, with more luck than he figured one person deserved, fallen in love again. Closing his eyes against the morning sunshine, he could hear his heartbeat pounding in his ears, and he tried to steady himself by taking slow, deep breaths.

"You know, Johnny," Fabian rumbled in his sleep-filled voice, "if you'd stop thinking so hard, you could sleep a little more." A hairy chest wriggled a little against his back, and he felt Fabian's hips move against his, a more than ample shaft sliding along his butt.

"It doesn't feel as though part of you wants to sleep," Jonathon said with a smile as he slipped his hand back between their bodies, fingers winding around the shaft in question, earning a soft moan and a nip on his shoulder just as the alarm on the nightstand began its morning chirp.

"Why did you set that thing?" Fabian groused, thrusting into Jonathon's hand when he tightened his grip.

"Because in a few days, you'll need to get used to getting up to go to work, and it's Saturday, remember? I promised to take your brother to the Prater." Jonathon rolled over, nudging a leg between Fabian's, their hips lining up. "This is a big step for him. The last few weeks before he starts university and begins to really take charge of his own life."

"I know," Fabian said, and Jonathon saw him look over his shoulder. "But it's only eight o'clock. He's not expecting us until eleven."

"Yes. That gives us an hour to get cleaned up and dressed, and two hours for…." Jonathon leaned forward, capturing one of Fabian's lips between his, tugging lightly as he slid his cock along Fabian's, and got a deep groan in response.

"I like the way you think," Fabian replied as Jonathon rolled him onto his back, pressing the younger man against the mattress. "And it just keeps getting better and better." Fabian returned the kisses, hands stroking down Jonathon's back.

"I certainly hope so," Jonathon added before kissing away the rest of Fabian's thoughts, replacing them with sounds one could only describe as urgently primal. And later, somehow, through some miracle from heaven, they actually managed to get cleaned up and dressed and downstairs just before Hans knocked on the door.

Jonathon opened it, surprised to see not only Hans but a girl with raven hair, huge eyes, and other voluminous assets. Hans had asked earlier in the week if he could bring a friend along, but Jonathon hadn't expected this friend to be a girl, and certainly not one as stunning as this one. *Go, Hans.*

"Come in," Jonathon said welcomingly, and the young pair stepped inside, with Hans holding her hand in his.

"Maria," Hans began, "this is my friend, Jonathon Pfister, and my brother, Fabian." Hans beamed. "This is Maria Hofschneider. We went to school together, and she'll be in my classes at university." Jonathon thought Hans was going to explode if he smiled any wider.

"It's very nice to meet you, Maria." He held out his hand, and the petite girl shook it with the grip of an Amazon.

"Thank you for allowing me to come." She looked at both Jonathon and Fabian before turning those huge eyes to Hans, who seemed to stand just a little taller than usual.

"You're very welcome," Jonathon answered as he motioned toward the door. "I thought we'd start at the Biergarten for lunch before taking in the attractions." Hans and Maria, still holding hands, led the way to the subway station, with Jonathon and Fabian following behind.

"Did you know about his girlfriend?" Fabian asked quietly, and Jonathon shook his head, suppressing a smile. "It seems my little brother isn't as shy and bookish as I thought."

Jonathon stopped walking for a second, letting the younger couple get a little farther ahead. "Your brother is smart, funny, and a real catch. He certainly isn't bookish, at least he hasn't acted that way with me. Besides, there's nothing wrong with being bookish," Jonathon added indignantly as he began walking again, a little faster now so they could catch up to the young lovebirds.

"I didn't say there was anything wrong with it," Fabian retorted defensively, and Jonathon flashed him a wicked smile. "Okay, you got me."

Reaching the subway station, they descended, and Jonathon paid his fare while the others used their passes. "Today is Hans's graduation present," he explained as he took his ticket and passed through the gate to the platform. It wasn't long before the train they needed picked them up and whisked them off toward the Prater station. Climbing the exit stairs, they emerged to a world of screams, laughter, clanging bells, and the whir of rides mixing with the music from the outdoor Biergarten.

Fabian led the way and got them a table for four. They started with mammoth glasses of beer before ordering their food. "Hans told me you're a teacher," Maria commented once they'd ordered.

"I teach eight- and nine-year-olds." Unsure of the translation to the European education system, Jonathon answered more generically. "Since you'll be in many of Hans's classes, are you studying to be an art restorer as well?"

She shook her head. "I don't have the patience for it like Hans does. I'll be studying art history and business so I can run an art gallery," she answered excitedly, and Hans looked at her, trying to hide his beaming smile behind the beer.

"Are you staying in Vienna long?" she asked, actually managing to sip daintily from the huge glass.

"I'm here for another month," Jonathon replied, glancing at Fabian. "Then I have to return to New York." He and Fabian hadn't talked about anything beyond the next few days, and he had no idea what Fabian's feelings were on the subject of him returning home. He had to go back if he wanted to keep his job. There had been a few times over the past few weeks where Jonathon had considered moving to Vienna. He had enough money to buy a place; that wasn't the issue. He needed to take the advice he'd given Fabian a few days earlier—he couldn't run away and hide. The change of scenery had done him a world of good, and he still had over a month, but in the end, he knew he'd have to leave. Jonathon felt Fabian's hand lightly pat and squeeze his knee, as though he could read his thoughts.

"I'd love to see New York. I've heard the art there is amazing." Maria looked at Hans. "Since studying abroad is part of the art program, maybe we could study in New York." Hans smiled back, completely smitten and ready to agree to anything she said.

Their food arrived and the conversation tapered off some, shifting to a discussion of the food, which was delectable. At one point Hans got up and excused himself. A few seconds later, Jonathon got up as well and followed him, stopping Hans just before he reached the men's room. "Hans," Jonathon called softly.

Accompanied by a Waltz

"Jonathon?" Hans looked uncomfortably confused.

"I've wanted to get you alone for a second since we left the house." Jonathon reached into his pocket. "I figured you and Maria would probably like to spend some time together." Jonathon handed Hans the bills he'd had in his pocket for him. "Show her a good time and don't tell anyone." Jonathon smiled and walked back toward the table.

Hans returned, and they finished their lunch. Leaving the restaurant, they gathered near the midway. "You two have fun." Jonathon smiled as the two young adults looked at each other with bright smiles before checking his watch. "We'll meet at the wheel before dinner and ride up together. So, have fun and ride everything you like." Jonathon watched with a smile as Hans and Maria walked toward the rides, her hand in his.

"They're adorable, aren't they?" Fabian breathed in his ear. "But not as adorable as a certain teacher I know."

Jonathon smiled. "Yes, they are."

"How much did you give him?" Fabian asked, and Jonathon hid his smile.

"That is none of your affair, but enough that they'll be occupied for hours." Jonathon took Fabian's hand. "Come on. Let's have some fun ourselves." Releasing the hand, Jonathon briskly walked away toward the rollercoaster. "You game?" Jonathon quipped as he bought two tickets and got in line, with Fabian right behind him.

They screamed and yelled as they plummeted and flew, bodies and souls taking flight as Fabian held Jonathon's hand through the entire ride, both of them grinning like kids when the ride came to an end. "What's next?" Fabian asked, grinning from ear to ear as they stepped back onto the ground, slightly queasy but definitely ready for more.

"The dodge-em cars," Jonathon cried with delight when he saw the sign. "Let's go." They stood in line and each got in their car. As soon as the power started, they all hurried around the track.

A bump from behind sent Jonathon careening into another car as Fabian whirred by. "Got you!" He was even cocky enough to wave—until he, too, was hit broadside and pushed into the wall, and then it was Jonathon's turn to laugh until he was hit again, and they both chuckled and cried out as they sped around the ring. When their time was up, Jonathon called over the attendant and paid for two more rounds. They bumped, ganged up on the other riders, laughed, and had the time of their lives. Getting off the ride, neither could walk straight, but neither cared as they moved to the next ride.

When neither could stand any longer from the whirling, climbing, and dropping, they both collapsed into one of the quiet gardens, letting their balance settle before helping each other to the Biergarten.

"Have you given any thought to what you'll do when you return to New York?" Fabian asked after the server plopped the beer onto their table under the trees.

"I don't know." Jonathon hadn't wanted to talk about this yet. "I'm going to miss this city," he teased.

"Just the city?" Fabian teased back, but Jonathon could see the hope in his eyes.

"No," Jonathon answered as he touched Fabian's hand. "Not just the city. But I don't know what the answer is." He knew he couldn't stay, and as much as he'd like it, he couldn't expect Fabian to leave his family and his home. It would be easier for Jonathon to stay—at least he didn't have any family—but he couldn't do that, at least not now. "We still have almost a month. Let's make the best of it."

"And when it's over, you'll go back to New York and leave me here, just like that!" Fabian raised his voice, and a few diners at another table looked at him for a second before returning to their own conversations.

"No, not just like that." Jonathon kept his voice low. "But what other option is there? Your life, your hopes and dreams, are worth no less than mine. I can't stay here, as much as I may wish it." Jonathon sat in the chair, staring down at his beer, suddenly completely uninterested in it.

"Fabian." Jonathon reached across the table. "Would you like to come to New York?" He'd asked, and Jonathon felt his heart thumping in his chest. "You don't have to give me an answer now, but I didn't want to assume anything."

"I...." Fabian stammered lightly. "I don't...."

"I know." Jonathon sighed when he saw the utter confusion on Fabian's face. "Your family is here, your life is here, and it's not fair of me to ask you to come back with me. Hell, I'm not even sure you could stay in the US if you wanted to. I have access to excellent lawyers, but...." Jonathon let his voice trial off. This conversation was definitely causing Fabian pain.

"That is not an issue. My mother's first husband, my father, was an Italian-American, and I have dual citizenship. Or at least I think I do. No one has ever pursued it. But I've only known my life here."

"I understand." Jonathon took a huge swig of his beer. Not that he'd been expecting a different answer, although Fabian's citizenship was an unexpected surprise. "Like I said, the offer's open, and you don't have to make a decision soon."

"Why can't you stay here?" Fabian inquired earnestly.

Jonathon found he didn't have a good answer, other than the fact that he knew he needed to go home. Even though he didn't relish the thought of going back to the home he'd shared with Greg, Jonathon knew he had to return, and he had to live there and move on. "It's hard to explain." He tried to put his feelings into words but found he just couldn't and have it make sense, so he took the simple route. "I love my job and love teaching, and I can't work here. My friends are there, my life is there—it's the same as it is for you here."

Fabian set his beer on the table. "You're right, but it does not make it hurt less."

"I know." Jonathon patted Fabian's hand. "And I'll understand if you don't want to continue seeing me." Jonathon could feel his chest clench as the words escaped his lips.

The bottom of Fabian's mug hit the table, sending beer sloshing onto the wood. "If you don't want me, then just say so." Fabian glared across the table and began to get up, eyes blazing with angry fire.

"I didn't mean that." Fabian stopped moving but didn't sit back down right away. "I only meant I would understand if you didn't. I know it's going to be hard to say good-bye when the time comes, and I meant that if you wanted to spare yourself the hurt, I would understand." God, he sincerely hoped Fabian didn't want that, and from his obvious hurt reaction, he didn't, but Jonathon had to give the younger man the out.

"No." Fabian lowered himself back into his chair. "I'm not a coward or a baby." Fabian's eyes still held some of their heat. "I would rather spend the next month with you and have you leave than run away from how I feel." Jonathon couldn't help noticing how Fabian threw his own advice back at him.

"Me too," Jonathon replied, letting a ghost of a smile cross his lips. During their conversation, he hadn't noticed the sounds around them—they'd faded as his entire attention had focused on Fabian—but as the tension between them waned, he once again heard the voices, laughter, and even the screams of the people all around them. Turning his chair slightly, Jonathon moved closer to Fabian as they finished their beer, watching people as they strolled under the trees.

Hans and Maria walked by but didn't see them, both completely oblivious to anything but each other. "I want some of that," Fabian said as he pointed to Hans and Maria. "I used to love candy floss."

Jonathon could almost feel his teeth ache. "If you'd like, when we're done here, we'll get you some cotton candy." Jonathon's eyes followed Hans and Maria until they walked out of sight. "Are you about done?" Jonathon asked as he drained the last of his beer. Fabian finished his as well, and they left the shaded Biergarten, joining the others as they strolled the walks.

"You up for the log flume?"

Fabian smiled wickedly as he nodded, making Jonathon wonder what he was up to. Getting in line, they bought tickets and waited their turn. At the front of the line, Jonathon climbed into the log, straddling the seat, and Fabian slid in behind him. A few seconds later, their log moved forward, and Jonathon felt Fabian press right behind him, arms curling around his waist. "This is what I call fun." He wriggled a little behind him, and then the boat began to climb, pitching him back against Fabian's warmth.

The bright sun greeted them as they climbed above the trees, floating on the channel of water as they moved over the park. The ride ended in a rush and a splash that left Jonathon wet and Fabian grinning. "So that's why you took the back." Fabian did his best to look innocent, but Jonathon knew better as he stepped off the ride, wringing the water from the tail of his wet shirt. At least his pants were mostly dry.

"I really didn't know you'd get so wet." Fabian grabbed his hand. "Come on, let's get you a dry shirt."

A few minutes later, they were standing inside a small shop, surrounded by souvenir shirts in every color and description. He found a simple blue one with "Vienna" embroidered on it and took it to the register with Fabian grinning behind him. "There's no way I'm wearing that." Jonathon pointed to the lime-green shirt with huge lettering in German and an arrow pointing up. He didn't know what it said, but he was sure it wasn't flattering. Fabian put the shirt back on the rack, and Jonathon paid for his purchase. Stepping around the side of the building, he pulled off the tags before taking off his shirt. "That's much better," Jonathon said with a smile as he shoved his wet shirt in the bag. Hands slid over his damp belly, leaving trails of warmth over his skin. "I need to put my shirt on."

The hands stopped on his belly. "I like you like this," Fabian cooed before stepping back, watching as Jonathon pulled the new shirt over his head. And they continued toward the Prater wheel, they saw Maria and Hans waiting near the entrance to the historic Ferris wheel.

Jonathon paid the nearly extortionist entrance fee, and they were ushered into one of the large, enclosed cabins, with Hans and Maria in the cabin behind. "Thank goodness," Fabian said as soon as the door closed and they'd moved forward. "I thought they were going to put them in here with us." Fabian took the seat right next to him and immediately kissed him hard, tongue demanding entrance. Hell, for a second, Jonathon thought Fabian was trying to climb him.

The wheel began to move again, loading more passengers, and Jonathon gasped as Fabian unhooked his pants, a hand winding its way inside. "I may only have you for the next month," Fabian hissed as Jonathon's head lolled against the seat, the sensation of Fabian's hand on him short-circuiting his brain, "but I intend to make it memorable." Jonathon felt his breath whoosh from his chest as he was surrounded in wet heat. The carriage rocked slightly as it moved and stopped again, while Fabian took him deep, throat clamping around him.

"Fuck, Fabian," he cried softly, forgetting for a moment where they were as Fabian's head bobbed on him, fingers tugging lightly on his sac. "Fabian, I can't… wait." All he heard was a mumble and then added pressure as Fabian sucked him hard and long, tongue twirling around the head just right. Gasping for breath, Jonathon tried to control himself as the wheel picked up speed. Fabian increased the suction as they bottomed out, speeding back toward the top. The pressure inside Jonathon's head matched the pressure building from the ride, and as they crested the top, weightless for a second, the pressure burst from deep inside, and Jonathon erupted as his head swam with ecstasy.

The wheel began to slow, and Fabian let him slip from his mouth, kissing him hard, and Jonathon somehow managed to get himself back together as the wheel pulled to a stop and their door opened. Without missing a beat, Fabian stood up and walked from the cabin, with Jonathon following behind on very wobbly legs. The attendant looked at them sideways as the next riders boarded the ride, and Jonathon thought he might have said something, but whatever it was, he couldn't understand. And then the kids got off a few seconds later, both of them with rather swollen lips.

"Are you two ready to head home?" Fabian asked.

"Yes," Hans answered with a smile as they fell in next to them, walking toward the exit. "Thank you, Jonathon," Hans said softly before falling back to Maria, taking her hand as they walked to the subway.

Accompanied by a Waltz

As they were exiting the subway near the house, Jonathon's phone rang, and he excused himself before fishing it out of his pocket, recognizing the number. "Greta?" he answered, mouthing to Fabian, "the nurse from the hospital."

"I hope I'm not disturbing you, but I wanted to call and let you know that the police have determined that Johan's real name is Reiner Kiesel, and he's from Berlin. I thought you would want to know."

"Danke schön. I appreciate the call." He heard her disconnect after saying good-bye, and Jonathon closed his phone. At least Johan had a name, and maybe someone could locate a family.

"Are you okay?" Fabian asked softly, and Jonathon nodded slowly, smiling at his lover as they continued the walk home.

"They found out who Johan, or more accurately, Reiner, really was. Kid grew up in Berlin."

"So he has a name," Fabian mumbled softly under his breath.

"Yes. Somehow it makes him more real. Somewhere, Reiner had parents, a family, maybe brothers and sisters," Jonathon commented softly. He couldn't help thinking about the young man. "It's hard to think that a person can die and there's nobody there for them."

"Who died?" Hans asked as they stopped at a street corner.

"The kid who was attacked near the house," Fabian answered, to Jonathon's gratitude.

"You mean the Strichjunge," Hans spat with an unusual amount of venom, and Maria elbowed him in the side. "Ouch," Hans cried as he rubbed his side.

"Every person deserves to be treated with a certain dignity and respect," Maria said as she stood just a little taller. The traffic stopped and they were able to cross the street. Jonathon knew he liked her.

"Why? Is it because of what Oma told you?" Fabian asked Hans, stopping on the other side of the street.

Hans nodded slowly. "Oma said you were with a Strichjunge and that's why you had to leave. She told us that whenever we asked about you while you were gone." The conversation switched to German, and Jonathon didn't understand any more of it, but he clearly understood Fabian's soft tone when he explained the truth, and it took no translator to interpret the relief on Hans's face and then the deep, brotherly hug that followed. Jonathon walked ahead with Maria as the two brothers cleared the air behind them.

When they reached the house, Hans escorted Maria inside to meet his mother and Oma, while Fabian followed Jonathon to the apartment door and then inside. "I was going to ask if things have been better on the Oma front?"

"For now, at least. The other night I heard her on the phone inviting her priest to dinner." Fabian shook his head. "Mutti is great and couldn't be more supportive, but Oma tries her best to make things miserable for everyone. Mutti threatened to move out, and since Oma can't take care of herself, Mutti said she'd put her in a home. That settled her down, so now she just ignores me."

"There are worse things," Jonathon said with a smile.

"Let's not talk about Oma," Fabian whispered as he moved closer. "What's wrong?" he prodded lightly when Jonathon didn't react.

"Sorry." Jonathon forced his attention back to the present and the man standing right next to him.

"Don't be sorry, just tell me what's got you so preoccupied all of a sudden."

"I will, but I don't think you're gonna like it." Jonathon was sure that Fabian was going to think he was completely and totally rollicking crazy. But Fabian just cocked his head at him quizzically, and Jonathon could almost see Fabian's mind going through possibilities. "I want to try to help Johan, er, Reiner."

"How? He's already…." Fabian's eyes widened, and Jonathon knew the minute he caught on. "No!" Fabian backed away.

"Fabian, he was killed, probably by his pimp, and you know the police aren't going to do anything about it. He was just another street kid. He's hardly a priority." God, Jonathon could feel the same helplessness he'd felt when he was on the street. He thought he'd left those feelings behind him long ago, yet here they were again—but this time those feelings weren't directed at himself, but at the young man whose hand he'd held while the life slipped from his battered body.

Fabian began pacing the kitchen floor. "What is it you think we can do?" Fabian asked, gesturing emphatically. "These men are dangerous, and I don't want anyone"—Fabian stopped walking, standing right in front of him—"especially you, getting hurt." The worried, almost pleading look in Fabian's eyes was almost enough to push the idea from his mind, but Jonathon just couldn't let it go.

"Those people killed that young man," Jonathon said slowly, his voice measured, "and they did it just down the street from where you live. I know you think it doesn't affect you"—he waved his arms toward the door—"I bet no one in the neighborhood thinks it affects them, because it was just a Strichjunge that was killed. You don't, Hans doesn't, why should anyone else? But they're wrong. What happens if Hans happens to be walking down the sidewalk and sees something he shouldn't?" Jonathon raised his eyebrows expectantly. "I know it's comfortable to think that it doesn't affect you and that it's outside your lives and experience, but it isn't." Jonathon couldn't tell if he was getting through to Fabian or not. Opening the refrigerator, he searched for something to eat, but he found next to nothing and shut the door.

"Maybe you're right, but what can we do about it?" Fabian asked as though that was the way it was. "Come on, let's go get something to eat," Fabian said. He walked toward the door with Jonathon walking just behind him, lost in his own thoughts. Locking the door behind them, they walked around the cars in the courtyard and out through the heavy gate, closing it behind them before heading down the sidewalk toward the restaurant where Jonathon and Fabian had eaten on their first date.

As they turned the corner, Jonathon nudged Fabian's side lightly, tilting his head toward the other corner, where a young boy stood leaning against the same wall where they'd first seen Reiner. Jonathon saw Fabian look, and the boy lowered his hand, sliding it along his belly, lifting his shirt to display the wares. "Let's keep going," Jonathon said slowly, and they walked the rest of the way to the restaurant in silence. Maybe there was nothing he could do, maybe he was just being a fool, but Jonathon knew he had to try, because Reiner's life was worth something—hell, his own life had been worth something.

At the door to the restaurant, Fabian stopped, and Jonathon found himself looking around. He could just see the corner where the boy stood, still just at the edge of the light. Tearing their eyes away, they went inside. Heinrich greeted them as he had on their previous visit, and they took their seats. "You're determined to do this?"

"Yes," Jonathon answered, opening his menu but not really seeing it as he watched Fabian disappear behind his own menu. Looking over the dishes, Jonathon made his selection and set the menu aside, waiting for Fabian.

"Okay." Fabian set his own menu on top of Jonathon's. "What do you propose to do?" he asked with a sigh of resignation. "I figure you'll do this on your own anyway, so I may as well help you." Fabian muttered other things under his breath, but they were in German anyway.

"We start by watching."

Fabian squinted at him from across the table. "Is that all?" Jonathon could see Fabian's body relax slightly.

"To start with." Jonathon looked toward the door. "Do you think we could sit outside?"

Fabian got someone's attention and they were moved to one of the umbrella-covered tables on the sidewalk. Jonathon shifted the table slightly, watching the corner. "Is that why you moved out here? So you could watch him?"

Jonathon reached across the table, taking Fabian's hand. "It's a nice night, and I'm here with you. I just wanted you to see something." The server returned and took their drink order. Jonathon kept his attention on Fabian, which was hardly a chore. He could look at this man for the rest of his life, and the realization surprised him a little, but in a warm, happy way. Their drinks arrived, and Jonathon took a sip of the light-colored beer. "Do you know what you'd like?"

Fabian nodded slowly. "You." The server took their order, and Jonathon felt Fabian's eyes on him the entire time.

A car drove past the restaurant and slowed down at the corner before continuing on. Jonathon placed his order, doing his best to pronounce the items correctly and earning a smile from Fabian. "Your German is getting better."

"I've been hearing it for almost a month," Jonathon replied as the same car passed by them again, and this time, Jonathon's attention wavered.

"What's got your interest?" Fabian turned, following Jonathon's gaze.

"That car passed us a few minutes ago. It slowed at the corner before continuing on. Now it's slowing again." Jonathon narrated the car's movements in a soft voice.

"But it didn't stop," Fabian added.

"Nope, but I bet it'll be back in a few minutes, and this time it will." Jonathon lifted his beer glass, watching Fabian over the top as he turned back to him.

"I will take that bet. But if you are wrong, you give up this whole notion."

"And if I'm right?" Jonathon didn't have time to say more before the car drove by them again, taillights brightening before pulling up to the curb. "See. Watch. They're negotiating the price right about now." Jonathon waited, and he saw a dark figure walk to the passenger door and get inside. "Offer accepted," Jonathon added knowingly as the car drove away. "That's the behavior of a customer. What we want is the big guy. He's probably the one who hurt Reiner."

"How do you know it was him? What if it was a customer?"

"Too early in the day. Besides, a customer would take him someplace more private, not in the street. No, the boss was sending a message to all his people not to mess with him or underperform." Jonathon swallowed. "I've seen it before." Jonathon cleared his mind, pushing away the memories as best he could, returning his attention to the exceptional man sitting across from him.

"So what are you looking for?"

Jonathon shrugged. "I'll know it when I see it."

"Then can we talk about something else?" Fabian's eyes widened, and Jonathon nodded, pushing everything away except Fabian for the rest of the meal.

On their walk home past the now-empty corner, Jonathon held Fabian's hand. "I have to talk to Mutti," Fabian told him as they approached the house. Jonathon let Fabian's hand slide from his as he made his way alone to his apartment. Closing the door behind him, he walked in the near dark up the stairs to the bedroom, stripping off his clothes and falling into bed alone, curling up on his side in the bed, wishing Fabian was on the other as he had been so many times recently.

Jonathon stared at the ceiling, wondering if Fabian was trying to get away from him. Not that he could blame him at all. He couldn't really put into words why he felt so connected to Reiner—he hadn't even met him other than to stand between the boy and Hans. He knew that he could easily have ended up like Reiner, but that wasn't quite it either. How could he expect Fabian to understand when he couldn't understand himself? He just knew he had to do this.

The door opening and closing downstairs made him jump. "Fabian?"

"Shhh, it's me," he heard the familiar voice answer, and after some fumbling in the dark, the bed dipped and Fabian joined him under the covers as relief flowed through Jonathon.

"I'm sorry for being such a problem," Jonathon whispered as Fabian moved closer, holding him in the darkness,

"You're not." Fabian tightened his embrace a little further. "I spoke to Mutti, and she said it was a good thing and that you were doing what was right." Fabian chuckled a little against his ear before nipping it with his lips.

"She said that?" Jonathon asked, and his answer was a kiss, slow and deep, as Fabian rolled on the bed, pulling Jonathon on top. "What else did she say?"

Fabian stilled, and Jonathon felt those deep eyes bore into him. "I asked her advice because you were going to leave. She said she only had my father for a short time before he died and that she wouldn't give up the time she had with him for anything. She suggested I make the most of the time I have with you." Fabian's mouth found his again as arms hugged him tight. "So that's what I'm going to do." Fabian kissed him again as they pressed their skin together, sharing warmth as the cool night air caressed them through the open window.

With surprising speed, Fabian rolled them on the bed, kissing Jonathon hard, tongue skimming over his lips. "You were so naughty on the wheel," Jonathon gasped as Fabian's mouth slipped away, his tongue circling a nipple.

"You liked that," Fabian moaned, his lips kissing Jonathon's skin. "You loved having sex outside, didn't you?" Fabian licked again, and Jonathon nodded against the pillow. "You loved that we might get caught—it really turned you on," Fabian teased lightly as he slithered down him, skin slowly skimming over his length. Jonathon gasped as Fabian increased the friction.

"Yes," Jonathon gasped as Fabian blew hot air over his length, his entire body throbbing with need. "Don't tease."

"Not teasing," Fabian countered. "Just getting you ready."

"For what?" Jonathon asked, fascinated, as Fabian's hands glided over his chest.

"A game. You can't make a sound, and I get to try to make you scream." Fabian licked his way up Jonathon's side, and he tried to squirm away, keeping his mouth tightly closed, swallowing the laughter that threatened. "Good. I'll be right back." Jonathon watched as Fabian crawled off the bed, hurrying downstairs, returning a few minutes later with a single candle, setting it on the bedside table. "I want to see you," Fabian whispered as he crawled back onto the bed, straddling Jonathon's legs.

Jonathon gazed up at Fabian in the flickering light, basking in the silent glow of those eyes. There was no doubt in Jonathon's mind how Fabian felt about him—it was plain, written on that handsome face with its chiseled jaw and impressive cheekbones. Reaching forward, Jonathon stroked a hand along the cheek, coarse, dark stubble passing under his palm. He wanted to tell Fabian how he was feeling, but he kept quiet, per Fabian's instructions.

Warm hands stroked along his chest, fingers splaying, and Jonathon arched his back, moving closer to the touch, skin tingling. Damn, the deep, kneading motion of Fabian's hands sent tingles throughout his body, and Jonathon's spirit soared as Fabian kept up his slow massage and Jonathon had to keep himself from groaning. Hands slid down his skin to his hips, and Fabian shifted, kneeling on the bed, fingers and thumbs stroking the long muscles of Jonathon's thighs and calves. Jonathon felt every stroke, every movement, as though the sensations were being written directly on his brain. Hip to toe, every inch of skin was touched, stroked, kneaded, stretched, and loved. Kisses followed those hands, and Jonathon felt his body sink into the mattress as every ounce of stress leached away through those magic, incredible hands.

The deep, soothing breaths they both took seemed to echo off the walls as Jonathon felt a light tap on his hip. Rolling over, he splayed himself on the bed, waiting for Fabian's hands to return, but he felt nothing, and it took all his willpower not to turn around to see what Fabian was doing. Instead he continued his deep breathing, jumping slightly when he felt fingers against his foot, thumbs deeply massaging the soles of his feet. Nothing in his experience prepared him for the zing that flew up his spine at the unexpected touch. "I know." Fabian's voice reached his ears as through a haze, and Jonathon opened his mouth to tell him how good it felt but closed it again, not wanting to do anything that would make Fabian stop.

The backs of his legs got the treatment next, muscles soothed, until Jonathon felt those incredible hands slide over his butt, hands working the muscles, fingers skimming along his cleft, and Jonathon felt himself press back slightly into the touch. With sweeping movements, Fabian moved upward, stroking down his back, over his butt, and along his legs before reversing course and returning, infusing him with desire as hips ground against the bedding. "That was just the beginning," Fabian said, and Jonathon felt hot breath against his skin. "You've made it so far," Fabian added, and Jonathon felt the hands slip back to his butt, wet heat tracing behind them. When that heat slid to his cleft, Jonathon swallowed the head-throbbing moan that tried to burst from him. "Like that?"

Jonathon nodded, not even trusting himself to breathe, let alone remain quiet. Fabian spread Jonathon's legs further, lips kissing along the inside of his thighs before sliding to his opening. Raising up on his hands, Jonathon felt his mouth fly open in a silent gasp as Fabian's tongue speared his opening like wet fire. Hands slipped around his sides, palms stroking his belly, as Fabian speared deeper, Jonathon's neck and head pulsing with every beat of his own heart. He had no idea how long he was going to last, and when Fabian's hand slid to his balls and under him, stroking along his shaft, he couldn't stop the backward thrust, grinding Fabian's face into him.

Somehow, he remained silent, but he knew he couldn't for much longer, and when fingers wrapped around his shaft, a long, slow moan ripped from his chest, filling the room and floating out the window on the breeze. Then everything stopped, Fabian's hands melted away, and the spearing heat dissipated. Gasping for air, Jonathon waited, his skin crying out for the contact it was now denied. "Fabian, please," was all he could manage between heaving breaths.

Rolling over to see what was happening, he felt Fabian's weight press over him, holding him down, covering him in warm security as their lips found each other, as Fabian's hips undulated above him, their cocks sliding against one another. Jonathon's eyes clamped closed as his body kicked into overdrive, completely overwhelmed by the wealth of sensation. Clinging to Fabian, he climaxed in a wave of gasping, mind-splitting, open-mouthed wonder.

His wrung-out body could barely move as Fabian continued his kisses, their sweat-drenched bodies clinging together. Jonathon felt Fabian's hands slide under him, arms holding them together as small mewls grew to outright groans, as Fabian's climax throbbed between them.

Fabian's weight shifted off him once they'd both caught their breath, and a towel, produced seemingly out of nowhere, passed over Jonathon's oversensitive skin before landing on the floor with a soft thud. With a soft puff, the candle went dark and Fabian resettled next to him, Jonathon holding the younger man tight. "Love you," Fabian whispered, and Jonathon's only response was to pull the younger man tighter, feeling like a heel that he couldn't say the words yet. Fear kept him from expressing what he already knew in his heart. He had to leave—soon—and while he knew it was silly, he felt as though actually saying the words would make the eventual separation harder for both of them. He should have known just how wrong he was.

CHAPTER Nine

DAYS and weeks passed faster than Jonathon could have ever imagined. "Fabian," Jonathon called as he heard his lover walk out of the bathroom one floor below, then heard his feet on the stairs. Throwing back the covers, he pulled his clothes out of the wardrobe, meeting Fabian at the top of the staircase.

"It is not necessary for you to get up with me every morning," Fabian said with a smile that told Jonathon he was happy about it nonetheless. They had less than a week before he had to return to New York, and Jonathon had determined a while ago that, though they might have to part, he was going to make the most of the time they had together, and if that meant getting up early to walk Fabian to the subway, that was okay with him. Fabian kissed him gently before dropping his towel, standing naked before bending to pull on his clothes, presenting that perfect backside. "Hey," Fabian gasped as Jonathon gave one of the cheeks a light pinch.

Jonathon chuckled as he leaned in, giving an apology kiss before pulling on his clothes and hurrying down to the bathroom. He cleaned up in a hurry and opened the door to find Fabian standing there, waiting for him with a goofy grin on his face. Jonathon didn't know what it meant until he was tugged close and kissed hard. "You really are special," Fabian told him softly as Jonathon returned the hug, resting his head on Fabian's shoulder.

"You're going to be late," Jonathon commented, but he really didn't want to stop what they were doing. It just felt so good. Finally, he released his lover and finished dressing just in time for them to leave the apartment.

The clouds overhead seemed to reach down between the houses, sending dampness through Jonathon's clothes as they walked across the courtyard and out through the gate. Approaching the corner, Jonathon saw the rent boy standing on the corner, huddled inside a thin jacket pulled tight around him. "What's he doing out at this hour?" Fabian asked as they passed. "I know you've been watching—I have too—but do you think we should let it go?"

Turning the corner, Jonathon forced himself to look away and watch where they were going. "Probably," Jonathon answered, knowing Fabian was right. It wasn't as though he was qualified to investigate Reiner's death. Over the last few weeks, he'd been paying special attention, but he hadn't seen anything he wouldn't have expected. He couldn't save the world, no matter how much he wished that the need for kids like the boy on the corner to sell themselves didn't exist. It did, and that was part of the way of the world.

"I know it hurts you and brings up memories you'd probably rather forget, but…." Fabian stopped walking. "Your caring nature is part of why I love you, and it's a big part of why I wish you would stay. Wish you could stay," he modified quickly.

"I know. I hate that I have to go, and I hate that you can't come with me." Jonathon stroked his hand down Fabian's arm, and he stepped closer.

"We have talked about this until we cannot talk anymore," Fabian began, "and we agreed to make the most of the time we have." His voice softened.

"I know." The words were on the tip of his tongue, to say that he'd get an apartment in Vienna and stay. But that would be only temporary. He couldn't work, and eventually his visa would run out and he'd have to go back anyway. Besides, he couldn't run away from his memories, no matter how much he wanted to. He had to go back, if for no other reason than to prove to himself that he could go back and live a normal life without Greg. Here, things were easy—there were no memories, and he was on a long vacation. But this wasn't his life, and this wasn't home, even if he wanted it to be. God, it was hard to explain even to himself, let alone anyone else. Thankfully, Fabian had understood, or at least he'd tried to. Jonathon was going to miss the beautiful man something fierce.

Fabian resumed walking and Jonathon followed, lost in his own thoughts. "I wanted to take you out tonight," Fabian said, breaking Jonathon out of his thoughts.

"That'd be nice," Jonathon answered as they approached the subway station. "I'll see you after work." Other people pushed around them, but Jonathon stepped closer, heedless of anyone watching, and kissed Fabian good-bye before watching him descend into the station.

Turning around, he began walking back to the apartment. It was still early, and while he had things he wanted to do today, he didn't have to be anywhere in a hurry. The dampness seemed to seep all the way into his bones, and the largely silent restaurant tables with their closed umbrellas only seemed to add to the gloomy mood of the day. Walking faster, Jonathon approached the corner and once again saw the boy, huddled as deeply in his jacket as possible. Jonathon watched him for a few seconds, not really wanting to draw his attention.

A deep rumble sounded from behind him. Turning around, Jonathon saw a huge Mercedes traveling fast, bouncing over the road toward him. Brakes sounded, and Jonathon saw the car come to a halt, and the kid moved toward the rear door. For just a few seconds, Jonathon caught a glimpse of the kid's face, lower lip curled between his teeth, eyes wide. His body was stiff. There was no doubt: this kid was near panic. A window lowered, and an unseen voice barked out something that made the kid jump and then move faster. This was the person Jonathon had been hoping to see, and he found himself staring, trying to see and hear more, but his own fear took hold.

A hand reached out of the window, yanking the kid close, slamming him against the side of the car with a thunk. Forcing his feet to move, Jonathon turned away and hurried down the street. But after taking a few steps, he forced himself to stop, turning back to see the hand from inside the car shove the kid away. His foot caught on the curb, and he fell backwards with a small cry. Another bark from inside the car, and the window silently lifted and the car began moving. Then it stopped again, the window lowering slightly, and Jonathon saw a pair of eyes peering out, looking at him. He couldn't suppress a shiver at the malice he felt in those few seconds. Forcing himself to lower his eyes and turn away, he walked slowly down the street as if he hadn't seen anything, hoping he hadn't roused the suspicions of whoever was in that car enough to follow him.

His feet feeling like lead, he forced his legs to move, and as he approached the gate, he glanced back and saw that the car was gone and the boy was picking himself up off the sidewalk. Looking around, Jonathon stepped through the gate, feeling like a complete and total coward. Closing it behind him, he walked to his door and slammed it behind him. God damn it, he could talk a good game about how important it was not to let people be victimized, but when it came time for him to do something about it, he couldn't even help the kid up off the pavement—he'd just run away. At least he'd gotten the plate information from the car, not that he knew what to do with it. Stepping to the table, he wrote it on a pad before climbing the stairs and flopping onto the sofa, thinking. Finally deciding what he needed to do, he picked up the phone.

"WELL, what did you expect?" Fabian asked as he sat down at the table. "A brigade of emergency vehicles descending on the neighborhood?"

"I know," Jonathon answered, handing Fabian a drink before joining him at the table. "I thought I was helping, but I guess it doesn't really matter." Jonathon looked down at the tabletop, sulking behind his glass.

A chair leg scraped the floor, and then hands slid over his shoulders and down his chest. "It does matter, to me. You watched and you gave the police the information, that's all you could do, and that's more than most people would." Fabian leaned closer, lips nibbling lightly on his ear. "Besides, we have a date."

Jonathon turned around to say something, and his mouth was immediately put to better use, Fabian's tongue sliding along his lip. "What should I wear?"

"Something nice, we're going dancing," Fabian breathed softly, kissing him again. "You did what you could, and for the rest of the night, you're all mine." Fabian's eyes danced, and Jonathon flashed on the way he used to look at Greg—it was just the way Fabian looked at him, and he wasn't sure if he should be happy about it or not.

"There's only us," Jonathon whispered, and he finished his drink before standing up. "I'll get dressed and meet you back here in twenty minutes." Jonathon climbed to the bedroom, hearing the door close as Fabian left. Opening the wardrobe, he pulled out the soft black pants and silk shirt he'd worn the night he and Fabian had gone to the opera. Slipping out of his jeans, he pulled on the supple pants and slipped the unbelievably smooth shirt over his skin. As nice as these fabrics were, they could never compare to the warm touch of Fabian's skin.

Sitting on the side of the bed, Jonathon finished dressing, hurrying down the stairs as he heard the door open and Fabian call his name. Jonathon stepped off the last step as Fabian turned toward him, looking stunning in his black tuxedo.

"I'm sorry," Jonathon apologized, looking down at his clothes. "I don't have a tux to wear."

Fabian moved closer, arms wrapping around his waist. "You look good enough to eat." Fabian slipped off his tie and draped his coat over the back of one of the chairs. "There, perfect," he responded, kissing Jonathon again. "Shall we go?"

Fabian led him to Oma's car, opening the door and waiting until he was seated before lifting the overhead doors and climbing into the car. As they backed out, Jonathon looked over at Fabian, wondering what the man had in store on what had turned into a beautifully warm, clear night.

Fabian drove to an area of town Jonathon wasn't familiar with, parking the car at the edge of what looked like a park. Opening the door, Jonathon could hear music, and Fabian smiled at him, leading him across the grass to a large open space surrounded by trees lit with fairy lights. At the far end of the clearing, a small orchestra warmed up as people milled around, talking and laughing.

"This is one of the best things about living in Vienna." The orchestra became silent, and a man stood in front and they began to play. "Everyone loves to waltz." Couples moved onto the large paved area and began to dance. Before he could say anything, Jonathon felt Fabian take him by the hand, leading him toward the dancers. At first he balked with self-consciousness, but one look in Fabian's eyes and his doubts fell away. Standing at the edge of the dance floor, Jonathon took Fabian's hand, put an arm on his waist, and swayed to the music before stepping out, joining the other swirling, flowing dancers.

"This is wonderful," Jonathon said as they moved to the sound of the music.

"Look." Fabian tilted his head to the far side of the square. "We're not alone." Jonathon looked and saw other couples like them, including an older couple who looked as though they'd been dancing together for decades.

"Thank you for bringing me here," Jonathon murmured against Fabian's ear as they broke their hold, moving closer, standing close together, the heat from their bodies passing from one to the other. "I…." Jonathon looked into Fabian's eyes, trying to say what was in his heart, but his voice failed.

"I know," Fabian answered, resting his head on Jonathon's shoulders as they moved together in one corner of the floor. The other dancers moved around them, but neither of them minded. Jonathon felt Fabian's lips touch his, and everything around them faded. Fabian's arms held him close as their bodies swayed and rocked, the small touches keeping the fires of desire on a slow simmer.

The small touches and sensual movements of the dance only added to the warm wanting Jonathon saw in Fabian's eyes and knew was reflected in his. Jonathon stepped back, and Fabian followed, their movements easily synchronizing until it became hard to tell where he left off and Fabian began. "I love you, Jonathon, and I want you to stay here in Vienna with me. I want that more than I've wanted anything in my life." Jonathon heard the hitch in Fabian's voice and knew the sentiment was absolutely sincere. The water at the edge of his eyes was enough to make Jonathon swallow hard, trying to keep his own emotions in check. Fabian tightened the grip on his waist, tugging him just close enough that he almost trod on Fabian's toes.

"I love you too," Jonathon whispered, not sure Fabian could hear him, but a small stumble told him he did. "And I wish more than anything that you could come back with me." There, he'd said it. No prevarication—he'd actually said what he felt. Not that he held out any hope that he'd get his wish. Fabian's family was here, and so was a job he loved, his whole life. Holding tight, Jonathon rested his head on Fabian's shoulder as his lover did the same. The music swelled and flowed around them, the other dancers swirling and moving in their Viennese waltz circles, but Jonathon needed something closer, more intimate. So he held his lover, their bodies swaying to the flowing beat, already starting to say his good-byes.

For what seemed like hours, they held each other as they danced. Voices sometimes intruded, but the interruptions were short, and they quickly returned to one another. In the wee hours of the morning, the music faded for the last time and the lights dimmed. Then and only then did they stop their movements, walking in silence to the car as the lights around the makeshift dance floor faded to black.

Jonathon settled in the passenger seat, watching Fabian as he climbed in the car, memorizing the mundane movements so he could remember everything once he left. They'd both said what they needed, and there was nothing else to be expressed on the subject, at least not now.

"How did you get Oma to let you use her car?" Jonathon asked as he stared out the window, not really seeing anything.

"She really is a loving person," Fabian replied. "She said if I was going to sin, I may as well do it in style." Jonathon saw Fabian's smile in the light of a passing car. "But if you want my opinion, I think Oma likes you, and maybe she's starting to try to understand." The flicker of hope in Fabian's voice made Jonathon's heart flutter a little. Fabian would be all right after he left. He had his family. Jonathon hoped he could say the same about himself, but he wasn't so sure.

Leaving the main road, Fabian threaded his way through the smaller streets before turning the last corner. Jonathon couldn't help looking to see if anyone stood in the circle of light at the corner, but it was empty, and Jonathon said a silent prayer that the boy was okay, cursing his cowardice under his breath but knowing at the same time there was nothing he could have done, at least not alone.

Fabian pulled to a stop and Jonathon got out, lifting the door and watching as Fabian pulled the car into the courtyard before stepping inside. He pulled down and latched the door, meeting Fabian outside his apartment.

Inside, Jonathon climbed to the bedroom with Fabian right behind, both knowing their way well enough that no lights were necessary. Standing next to the bed, Jonathon felt the heat from Fabian's body before their mouths found each other. Clothes quickly melted onto the floor, hands caressed backs, lips trembled. Falling backwards, Jonathon bounced slightly on the bed until Fabian's weight stilled him. Warmth spread throughout his body, warmth fueled by Fabian's heat on the outside and their passion on the inside.

Fabian's mouth slipped away from his, and a scorching wetness circled a nipple before lips clamped onto his skin, sucking lightly, and Jonathon felt more than vocalized a moan that began in his toes. Threading his fingers through Fabian's hair, he did his best not to mash his lover's face against his skin, wanting more sensation but wanting Fabian to take his time too. Bringing their mouths together, Jonathon devoured his lover, exploring deep, committing everything to memory. After releasing the kiss, Jonathon felt Fabian's mouth on his neck, tongue licking, lips sucking lightly, tingles running down to his feet. "You may be leaving," Fabian breathed into his ear, "and the mark will fade, but know I will still love you." Fabian's tongue soothed over the abused skin before licking its way lower, swiping over each nipple before he kissed his way down Jonathon's stomach, hands following right behind the lips, Jonathon throbbing on the mattress with every touch.

Hissing softly as Fabian's lips ghosted along his shaft, hips thrusting forward on their own, Jonathon felt Fabian's tongue glide around the head before he sucked him deep, sliding along his length. "Fabian!" Jonathon tried to stop the cry but couldn't. Trembling against the sheets, gripping the bedding in clenched fists, Jonathon managed to keep control of himself, not wanting Fabian's exquisite torture to end. Then the heat slipped away and Jonathon heaved a deep breath, letting his hand swipe the sweat from his brow.

"Jonathon," Fabian whispered into the near-complete darkness as Jonathon felt his weight again. "I want you." Fabian's hand traveled down his hip and beneath a cheek, fingers teasing along his cleft.

Jonathon swallowed hard, nodding slowly against Fabian's lips. "Yes," he answered, hands sliding to Fabian's jaw, bringing their mouths together in a searing kiss. Fabian's knees parted his legs, and Jonathon wrapped them around Fabian's waist.

"When was the last time?" Fabian asked, and Jonathon found he couldn't answer. He didn't want to talk or even think about Greg while he was with Fabian. That wasn't fair. "Oh," Fabian added into the silence before kissing him again and slinking down his body, lips and tongue retracing their familiar trail.

Taking the gentle tap on his hip as a signal, Jonathon rolled onto his stomach, feeling Fabian's lips on his shoulder, down his back, a slight nip on one cheek, then the other. Hands kneaded him, fingers teasing their way down his cleft, making Jonathon's breath catch as Fabian's tongue blazed trails of liquid fire behind those fingers. Breath that was released with a gasping cry when that tongue reached his opening. It had been so long, and Fabian knew just what he was doing, and.... Jonathon gasped again, crying out softly as Fabian's tongue stabbed him, filling him with exquisite heat that raced all the way to his throbbing temples. "Fabian... please, God!" He was babbling and he knew it, but he just couldn't stop—not that he wanted to anyway.

Jamming his hips into the air, Jonathon felt Fabian's face mash against him, going deeper, a stubbled jaw grinding against his tender flesh.

"Gotta get you ready," Fabian soothed, a hand stroking over his scraped skin.

Waiting, praying for something to happen, Jonathon heard no sound except their breathing, felt no movement on the bed. Then a small snap as something opened. A finger, hot and slick, drew small circles on his skin, re-igniting the desire. A fingertip pressed inside, making small circles of heat within.

"Fabian."

"Shhh, just taking my time," Fabian cooed, and Jonathon felt the cursing begin in his head.

"I'm not made of glass, damn it!" Jonathon growled, and Fabian simply chuckled.

"You are to me." The finger went deeper, and Jonathon sighed softly. "To me, you are fragile and worth taking care with."

Jonathon's head throbbed and his body jerked as Fabian found the bundle of nerves, sending shocks of pleasure through him again and again. As one finger was joined by another, Jonathon felt the stretch and slight burn that quickly dissipated, morphing into something incredible. "How do you want me?" Jonathon asked as the thick, filling fingers began a slow retreat. When Fabian didn't answer, Jonathon rolled onto his back and waited, listening to the small, familiar preparatory sounds.

"Just like this," Fabian answered softly as he set Jonathon's ankles on his shoulder, his thickness pressing against Jonathon's opening. Breathing deep, Jonathon waited before feeling Fabian press forward, his body opening as Fabian slowly filled him. "Won't hurt you," Fabian reassured him as he pressed further, sliding deeper.

After what seemed like hours of agonizing slowness, Jonathon felt Fabian's hips against him. They were joined, and he waited, feeling Fabian throbbing inside him. Hands stroked along his skin, fingers wrapping around his length, stroking him back to full hardness.

Jonathon strained to see through the darkness, but only Fabian's silhouette became visible no matter how he strained his eyes. So, giving up, he lay back against the pillows as Fabian began to move. Long, slow, full movements followed, each and every one felt from head to toe. Gasps and cries filled the room, startling him when Jonathon realized they were his. It had been a long time. For too long, he'd denied a part of himself, holding it back, but with every movement, every stroke, every filling thrust, Fabian broke down his last remaining walls. Jonathon knew it would hurt when he had to leave in a few days, but as his release built, he realized the hurt he'd experience was nothing when weighed against the joy Fabian had brought. "So close," Jonathon cried, letting everything else go but him and Fabian.

"I know," Fabian moaned softly. The pressure on his shaft increased, Fabian's fingers tightening, the soft, slapping sound of skin on skin increasing as the bed rocked with their movements. God, this man played him like a fiddle, and Jonathon squirmed under his touches, needing more while at the same time afraid of a sensory overload.

Jonathon thought his head might explode as his climax rushed upon him like a freight train, carrying him away as he clamped his eyes closed, riding the orgasmic high for all it was worth, his spirit taking flight.

It took a while, but slowly, he came back to himself, panting hard. Fabian waited, motionless, and Jonathon expected him to move again, but instead he pulled out slowly. Jonathon heard his lover's panting, realizing he'd still been zoned out when Fabian came. The bed jiggled, and Jonathon heard footsteps padding across the floor and down the stairs. The one thing about this apartment was that it needed a second bathroom. Listening, he heard Fabian return, and after a quick cleanup of both of them, Fabian rejoined him on the bed, where they held each other tight, exchanging kisses.

Jonathon felt his eyelids droop, his body aching for sleep, but he pushed it away, at least for now. Squirming away, he rolled over and turned on the small light before fishing around in the drawer. "I got you something," Jonathon said as his hand brushed against the small box he was looking for. "I was going to give it to you later, but I want you to have it now." Jonathon turned back to Fabian and handed him the box. "I wanted to get you something to remember me by, and when I was wandering around, I found a coin shop. He had all kinds of things, but I found something that reminded me of you."

Jonathon watched as Fabian opened the box, peering inside. "It's a Roman coin. I bought two and had them mounted by a jeweler for each of us. That way when I see mine, I'll think of you, knowing you have the only other one like it."

Fabian held up the chain, the coin in its mount twisting, glinting in the low light.

"Look at the back of the mount," Jonathon instructed.

"It's the Austrian eagle," Fabian breathed.

"Yes, I also had the year added." Jonathon swallowed and watched as Fabian burst into a smile.

"Thank you, Johnny. I'll treasure it always." Fabian set his gift back in the box, placing it on the table before pulling Jonathon into a deep embrace. "It's very special, just like the man who gave it to me." Jonathon heard the hitch in Fabian's voice and turned off the light, knowing they were both very close to tears. Holding Fabian tight, he relished the feel of being held, knowing that in a few days he'd have to leave. Jonathon knew tonight was the beginning of the good-bye process, and over the next few days, they'd do a number of things for the last time. He also knew that, each time, it would get harder and harder. Rolling over, spooning himself to Fabian's back, he held his younger lover tight and reluctantly let sleep take him.

CHAPTER Ten

First class or not, Jonathon got off the plane tired and wrung out. Walking down the jet bridge, he found his hand traveling to his throat, feeling the coin that rested in its mount next to his skin. When he'd left the apartment to go to the airport, Fabian had waited for him near the car, and to Jonathon's surprise, the rest of his family was there as well, even Oma. Hanna had hugged him tight, asking him to please come back. Hans had stood tall, shaking his hand like an adult, telling him he'd e-mail and had already friended him on Facebook. "Maria said to tell you good-bye and thank you," the young man had added before swallowing and turning away.

Oma had taken both of his hands, smiling at him. "You a good boy," she'd said, squeezing his hands before releasing them and following Hans back into the house. Hanna said one last good-bye before leaving him and Fabian alone.

"We should go or you will be late," Fabian said softly, emotions warring behind his eyes. Jonathon nodded and got his bags, placing them in the back. Fabian closed the hatchback, and Jonathon slid into the passenger seat of the gumball machine. They rode in near silence, Fabian driving intently, Jonathon sitting numbly, trying not to feel or think about anything.

At the terminal, they unloaded his bags onto the curb and stood, looking at one another. Most everything had already been said the night before. Finally, Jonathon pulled Fabian into a hug, holding the man tight, fingers threading through the hair on the back of Fabian's head, not wanting to let him go. "Fabian, I...." Jonathon faltered as he tried to talk around the huge lump in his throat. There were suddenly so many things he wanted to say, but they all seemed clichés, and it seemed ridiculous to say them now that he was leaving.

"I know," was Fabian's only response as he kissed him, hard, for just a second and then backed away, wiping his eyes once before walking around the car and opening the door. Fabian raised his hand in a final good-bye before climbing into the car and shutting the door. Jonathon watched as the car pulled away and waited for its taillights to get lost in traffic before picking up his suitcase to enter the terminal.

Now, reaching the end of the jet bridge, he passed through the doorway and entered the flow of traffic heading toward baggage claim, his carry-on bag already heavy on his shoulder. He'd tried to nap on the plane, but it hadn't worked, and he'd spent much of the flight either reading or watching movies that he barely paid attention to. His mind refused to settle on anything except Fabian, and that was the one thing he didn't want to think about.

Taking the escalator down, he found himself standing in the passport line. Waiting, he looked around and watched people until it was his turn. The agent looked at his papers, checked his picture, and scanned the passport before handing it back to him and moving on to the next person. Moving to baggage claim, he waited again, pulling his bag off the carousel and walking to the customs line, where they sent him to another table. "Great," he muttered under his breath as he stepped to the counter, handing the agent his paperwork.

A woman in a blue uniform looked over his paperwork, asking a few questions before pulling on a pair of gloves and opening his suitcase. She checked things carefully before repacking and closing the suitcase. "Thank you," she said again, and Jonathon picked up his things and walked through, riding the elevator upstairs and finally making his way outside. Instantly, the scent of the city assailed him as he waited in line for a taxi that would take him home.

The taxi pulled up to the house, and Jonathon heaved himself off the seat. Getting out, he paid the driver and carried his luggage toward the door. Everything looked the same—the garden service had done a nice job keeping things clean and neat. Opening the door, he set down his bags and stepped to the patio doors, throwing them open, letting in fresh air and the sound of the ocean below. Standing by the rail, he inhaled deeply, glad to be home.

His phone ringing pulled him out of his thoughts, and he fished it out of his pocket, recognizing the number. "Fabian." He couldn't help smiling. "I just made it home." Some of the sadness drifted away.

"Was everything okay?"

"Yes." He wanted to say more, tell Fabian he missed him and had thought of him the entire trip home, but he didn't. He couldn't. There was nothing either of them could do about it, and there wasn't any use in making Fabian miserable. Besides, what if he didn't feel the same way? Jonathon didn't think he could take that right now. No, it was best to leave things as they were and let the trip become a fond memory. "Everything's fine." The ocean breeze caressed his face as he talked, as if reassuring him that he'd made the right decision.

"I called because we had a visit from the police this evening. They were looking for you." Fabian's voice sounded ominous.

"What did they want with me?"

"They caught the man who killed Reiner," Fabian answered. "It seemed your watching and the call to the police with the plate number was a help. They didn't say much more, but I wanted to let you know." Fabian became quiet for a few seconds.

"Thank you for telling me." Jonathon didn't know what else to say. "I need to get unpacked, and it must be late there." God, he sounded so stiff. How could he have spent weeks with the man, slept with the man, and yet have nothing to tell him over the phone?

"It is," Fabian said.

"Schlaf gut," Jonathon said, remembering his German.

"Good night," Fabian said. "Du fehlst mir," he added quickly before hanging up.

Jonathon stared at the silent phone for a second wondering just what Fabian had said, but the words really didn't register. Putting the phone back in his pocket, he sighed, thinking of what he had to do, and figured he may as well get to it. Not yet ready to tackle the mountain of mail on the dining room table—Marty had seen to everything important anyway—Jonathon picked up his suitcases and walked to the bedroom.

It looked the same as it always had; in fact, it looked identical to how it had when Greg was alive, and Jonathon felt stifled, realizing just how alone he still was. Flopping the suitcase on the bed, he opened his drawers and began the process of unpacking, throwing all the dirty clothes in the hamper. At least it gave him something to do for all of half an hour. Putting the suitcase away, he'd just started the laundry when the doorbell rang.

"Marty!" Jonathon called as he opened the door, hugging the man tightly before inviting him inside.

"Here's your key," his friend said, laying it on the table by the door. "How was Vienna?"

"Wonderful," Jonathon answered, remembering Fabian and smiling. Marty looked at him, a little bewildered, but said nothing. "Thank you for taking care of things."

"It was no trouble, you know that," Marty said, still looking at him strangely. "You look different, more peaceful. I think being away did you some good." Marty looked back toward the door. "I really can't stay, we're on our way out, but I saw you were home and wanted to drop in." Marty walked toward the door, his hand on the knob. "Let's go to dinner later in the week. I can't wait to hear about your adventure."

"Great. I'll call you in a few days, once I'm settled." Jonathon watched as Marty waved before closing the door, and Jonathon saw him walk in front of the windows as he headed back to his car.

Sitting at the table, Jonathon began sorting the mail. It wasn't long before he'd pulled the trash can to the table, sorting the better part of it right into the garbage. Gradually, the quiet surrounded him, broken only by the sound of the washing machine and the motor on the refrigerator cycling on and off. Finishing with the mail, he walked into the kitchen and dug out a delivery menu. After placing a call for Chinese, he wandered into the bathroom to clean up.

As he started the water for his shower, the phone rang again, and he almost let it go to voice mail before relenting and answering.

"Dad!"

Jonathon smiled. "Jeana, how are you? Where are you?"

"I'm fine, and I'm in Vienna. We must have just missed you."

"Oh," was all he could think to say. He wanted to ask her about Fabian but restrained himself. Any questions would only give her license to interfere, and things were better off as they were.

"We're here just overnight, and tomorrow I'm going to Paris to catch a flight to New York. So I'll see you in a couple days." She sounded so excited, and Jonathon felt it too. "I'll be home for a few weeks, and then I need to come back for classes."

"You could just stay." It really wasn't necessary for her to come all the way back for just a few weeks.

"No. I need some time at home before classes start."

"Are things okay with Inge?" Jonathon asked, hoping she wasn't coming home to nurse a breakup.

"They're great. I just wanted to spend some time with you, okay?"

"Yes." Jonathon could already feel himself looking forward to it. He'd only been home a few hours, and already the walls were closing in. "I'm going in to school tomorrow. I need to get my classroom ready. And I was thinking I'd add some lessons on Europe for Social Studies this year." He needed something to do, and he actually felt a touch of anticipation.

"Sounds great, Dad. I'll see you in a few days." Jonathon heard her yawn and said good-bye before hanging up. The doorbell rang almost immediately. Pulling on some pants, he hurried to the door. After paying the delivery girl, he ate his dinner standing at the breakfast bar.

Stomach full, Jonathon returned to the bathroom and took his shower before pulling down the covers and climbing into bed. Lying beneath the cool sheets, he stared at the ceiling, completely exhausted but not able to sleep. Turning on his side, he found himself staring at the clock. He thought of Greg and their years together, those memories a warm glow that brought a smile to his face. As he continued lying in bed, he thought of Fabian, and the ache that had remained on the periphery all day came racing to the front. He missed him terribly. Yes, he was home, but it felt just as lifeless as it had when he had left. The apartment in Vienna, small as it was, had never felt lifeless, not for a second. Listening, Jonathon heard the sound of the ocean through his window, waves breaking regular and steady, but not a voice. No cars, no people passing on the sidewalk, no sounds of life. Even when he'd been alone in the apartment, he hadn't felt alone. There was always life just outside the door waiting to pull him along with it. Finally, after lying awake for hours, Jonathon fell into a fitful sleep.

JONATHON pulled into the driveway and pressed the button to raise the garage door, smiling to himself. He'd spent much of the last two days getting his room ready for his students, and he was really pleased with his progress. He'd shown some of his pictures to the principal, who had loved the idea of doing a series of lessons on Europe and had even agreed to share some of his pictures and experiences. The kids would start in a week, and he'd already planned to go to the lake for Labor Day weekend. It could be his last chance before winter, and he really wanted—no, needed—the time to think. Pulling into the garage, he stopped the car and saw the door to the house open, and Jeana walking into the garage. By the time he'd closed his car door, she had him in a brutal hug that had never felt better.

"I was wondering when you were going to get home." She released him and stepped back. "You've been working like crazy, haven't you?" she asked as she walked back toward the open door, pushing the button to close the overhead door. "I bet you've already got your classroom ready."

"Nearly." Jonathon chuckled, following her inside. "Where's your car?"

"I sold it before I left. There wasn't any use keeping it, since I was going to be gone for almost a year." She walked into the kitchen, and Jonathon smelled something wonderful. "I was hoping to use Dad's car when I was home."

Jonathon opened the drawer near the sink, pulling out a set of keys. "I can do one better." He handed her the keys. "It's yours now. Your father babied that car, and I've driven it a little to keep it running, but I don't need two." Jonathon smiled at her unabashed surprise. "He'd want you to have it."

"You're giving me his Mercedes?" she asked in what sounded like total disbelief.

"Yes. It's time I moved on. I also asked Marty to arrange to have the Lake George house transferred to you and your brothers. That's what your dad would have wanted. It was his grandparents', and it should stay in the family." Jonathon watched as she worked at the stove. "I'll let you decide how you want to tell them."

Jeana stopped stirring. "After all they put you through, you still did this for them?"

"It was always for you kids anyway," Jonathon said as he walked to the cupboard to set the table. "You didn't have to cook."

"Of course I did. I wasn't in the mood for takeout." She grinned and motioned toward the trash. "I swear you'd eat takeout every night if I wasn't around. You cooked when you were in Vienna. You could do it when you're home too." Jeana turned down the heat under the sauce and put the pasta on to cook. "This is quick and easy anyway. I just started with jar sauce and doctored it." She stirred the pasta, and Jonathon felt her watching him.

"What is it? If you keep looking, you'll stare a hole in my back."

"Aren't you going to ask about Fabian?" Jeana said as she tapped the spoon against the edge of the pot.

Jonathon set down the last plate, keeping his back to her and nearly jumping out of his skin when she touched him. "I don't want to talk about it, Jeana." She said nothing, and he turned around before heading to the bathroom, closing the door and standing in front of the mirror, staring at himself, watching.

Jeana's voice floated through the door. "Dinner's ready."

"I'll be right in," Jonathon called, wiping his eyes with a tissue before throwing it in the trash and walking back to the dining room. "This smells wonderful," he said, trying to change the subject as she brought in the serving bowl and some garlic bread. "Thank you." He dished up their plates and began to eat.

"I know you don't want to talk about it, so I'll talk." Damn, the girl was so much like her father—pushy as hell. "Fabian's miserable. All he did was mope around and talk about you." She took a bite and swallowed. "It was sort of pathetic since you left him."

"Jeana." His voice sounded sharper than he intended, and he did his best to soften it. "It was for the best. He has a good job and a life in Vienna. My life and job are here." He set down his fork. "It was hard to leave, but I had to. It was time to go home." Jonathon took a drink of his ice water. "Not everything works out like in the movies," he whispered, wishing so very hard that it did. "Can we please talk about something else?"

"Sure." Jeana stared at him for a long time and then began telling him about all the places she'd been to and what she'd seen. Jonathon listened intently to her stories and for a while forgot about his own worries as they talked and laughed together. After they'd eaten, Jonathon cleared the table and did the dishes before spending the evening trying to read, but his mind just wouldn't cooperate.

Closing his book with a thud, Jonathon set it on the table. He'd read the same page three times and couldn't remember a freaking thing. Getting up, he walked outside, standing on the deck, staring out over the water, watching as the last glimmers of light flashed off the waves and then disappeared, the sky going from hints of red to purples and then black in just a few minutes.

"You okay, Dad?" he heard Jeana ask from behind him, and he nodded without turning around. "I'm going to bed. I'll see you in the morning," she added, and Jonathon turned, giving her a hug.

"Good night," Jonathon said softly, and he watched as she walked toward her room before he turned back to stare out at the nearly complete, inky blackness of the water, feeling the darkness reach deep into him. "What have I done?" Jonathon asked himself softly, barely forming the words.

Closing his eyes, he let his mind wander as the cool breeze blew over his skin. Almost immediately, his mind's eye conjured up the evening in the park as he and Fabian danced under the stars. Jonathon could almost hear the music and see the lights twinkling in the trees. His body swayed slightly as the music played in his head, Fabian's hand touching his, feet stepping, moving together, their bodies, each an extension of the other, moving as one. Jonathon could almost feel the intensity in Fabian's eyes, looking deep inside him, as they made love with their clothes on. His eyes flew open as his hip bumped the railing. He hadn't even realized that he'd started dancing until he came back to his senses. Shaking his head, glad Jeana hadn't seen him, he once again returned his attention to the water, sighing softly. Moonlight now bounced off the waves, the water shining in the night.

Turning around, Jonathon closed the patio door behind him before wandering through the house, turning off the lights before climbing into bed.

HEFTING the suitcase, Jonathon placed it in the trunk before closing the lid. Walking back in the house, he mentally checked his list, making sure he had everything as he checked the rooms one last time, stopping in the living room, looking at the fireplace. He almost reached up and took Greg's urn from the mantel, but he stopped himself with a smile. He didn't need it anymore. Greg was with him all the time now, and he was happy with that. Turning, he bumped into Jeana, almost knocking her over as she passed in front of the doorway. "Sorry," he said, and she mumbled something unintelligible on her way to her first cup of coffee. He heard her pour her mugful, followed by a soft sigh.

"Feeling human?" Jonathon said teasingly, knowing he was exactly the same way.

"Yes," she breathed, taking another sip.

"Are you coming to the lake? If so, you need to get your things in my car."

Jeana shook her head, wandering toward the deck. "I've got some things I need to do this afternoon, and I'm meeting some friends this evening in the city before I go back to Europe on Wednesday, but I'll be up tomorrow before lunch." She continued drinking her coffee, seeming more alert.

"The kids have a half-day today, so I'll be leaving early, right from school," Jonathon explained as he picked up his case, getting ready to leave. "I'll see you tomorrow. Be sure to lock up everything in the morning."

"Don't I always?" she retorted, rolling her eyes before setting down her mug and giving him a hug. "See you tomorrow, Dad," she said with a smile before picking up her coffee and wandering toward her bedroom. Jonathon left the room, closing the door behind him. Opening his door, he sank into the white leather seats of his car, pressing the button to raise the garage door before backing down the driveway.

After arriving at school, he got out, locking the doors and walking into the building through the metal detectors, going directly to his classroom. Since it was a half-day, he'd planned something fun and had even gotten the other third-grade teacher to help. Karen had been teaching her kids about France for years, and they decided to work together and expand the lessons to more of Europe and include both classes.

Making sure everything was ready, Jonathon wandered to the teachers' lounge.

"Hey, Jonathon." Duane, one of the sixth-grade teachers, approached. "I understand you have the gym reserved."

Jonathon finished pouring his coffee. "Yes. Since it's a half day, I thought I'd do something special. Why?"

"Just wondering how you finagled extra gym time."

"I didn't. We're using it for a lesson that takes a little extra space," Jonathon answered quietly, trying to keep the peace. He looked at the clock, thankful to see he had five minutes before the kids started arriving. "If I don't see you, have a great holiday weekend," he added to the room in general before heading for the door, making a beeline to his room, gulping his coffee as he went.

Reaching his room, he did a final check as the bell rang. After finishing his coffee, he put his mug in his desk and listened to the sounds of an army with tiny feet and small voices. Wandering into the hall, he watched as the kids got out of their jackets and began to file into the room. Once the second bell rang, he closed and locked his door before calling the class to order and taking attendance.

The kids were wound up and excited. "Put your things in your desks and line up at the door." Desks opened and closed, voices raised. "Quietly," he reminded them, and the talking ended. When they were lined up, Jonathon opened the door and led his class down the hall to the gym, with the other class right behind.

He had the kids sit on the floor in a small group. "We've started studying Austria, and Mrs. Coleson and I thought we'd do something special. One thing that is very important in European culture, particularly in Vienna, is dancing. But not just any dancing—waltzing."

"So," Karen took over, "Mr. Pfister and I are going to teach you how to waltz."

Some of the kids jumped to their feet, already excited, while others tried to hide. Karen walked to the CD player. "We're going to demonstrate for you," Jonathon explained, and the music started. Taking Karen's right hand, he placed his other on her hip and began to step to the beat of the music, a simple waltz. Counting out loud, Jonathon exaggerated his steps and let the kids watch. When the song ended, they stepped apart. "Everyone stand up." The kids climbed to their feet, and two of the girls raised their hands.

"Yes, Susie?"

"I learned this in dance class," she said a little timidly.

"Has anyone else learned?" Jonathon asked, and a few raised their hands, Jonathon motioning the girls forward. The music started, and the girls began moving through the basic steps, holding their arms out to imaginary partners.

"Very good," Karen applauded when the song ended. Pairing the kids off took a few minutes, and then Karen spent the next half hour walking the children through the steps. Some did well and some had two left feet, but everyone seemed to have fun.

Checking the clock, Jonathon noticed that they had less than half an hour before the dismissal bell. "Would you like to see how they dance in Vienna?" The children applauded, some jumping up and down. Jonathon held out his hand, and Karen walked to him.

"I've never done this before," she said quietly.

"Just follow my lead and you'll be fine." He started the music, and Strauss's "Tales from the Vienna Woods" began. Waiting through the introduction, Jonathon swayed with his partner, setting the rhythm, and they stepped into the dance. Immediately, the gymnasium, the children, Karen, everything fell away, and Jonathon was transported back to Schönbrunn, seeing once again the surprised expression on Fabian's face when he'd led the man around the dance floor.

A misstep by his partner shattered the illusion, slamming into him almost like a physical blow. Forcing himself to continue moving, he brought them to a stop. "Are you okay?" Karen asked him under her breath, and Jonathon nodded, stepping away and turning off the music, using the time to take deep breaths to clear his head.

"Did you like that?" Karen asked, and the children hooted and screamed, jumping enthusiastically.

"Line up," Jonathon said, and the children separated into classes, lining up in front of their respective teachers for the short trip back to the classroom. In the room, there wasn't much time left, and Jonathon had the children sit quietly until the bell rang, and then pandemonium broke out until they were out the door.

"Jonathon, was something wrong?" Karen poked her head through the door. "When we were dancing, you seemed far away, and you had this dreamy look in your eye." Karen lowered her voice. "Wherever you were, I want to go there too." She gave him a quick smile and returned to her room. Jonathon cleaned up the room, packed his lesson planner in his bag, and left the room, shutting the door behind him.

Walking through the nearly empty hallway, he returned greetings and waves, stopping in the office briefly to check his mailbox before walking outside and to his car. The sun warmed his skin as he opened his car door, slipping behind the wheel. Watching for children and other teachers, he backed out and pulled onto the street.

Hours, a few stops, and many miles on freeways and a two-lane highway later, Jonathon turned into the small village of Raquette Lake, tired and excited at the same time. Parking his car near the boat dock, he shut off the engine and got out. Standing by the door, he inhaled deeply, the scent of the water filling his nose. Walking across the gravel lot, he stepped into the general store, buying a few provisions and, of course, the to-die-for doughnuts.

It took some time to get the boat uncovered and all his things transferred, but then he was on the lake, motoring northward past coves and camps, through the needles and on to the far side of the lake, stopping at his dock. Jonathon got everything unloaded and dinner made just in time for him to eat it sitting on the porch, watching the sun dip behind the trees surrounding the water. The temperature continued to drop, and Jonathon went inside, got a thick quilt to wrap around his shoulders, and returned to his porch, sitting, listening, and thinking. The tension from the city fell away, but there was a part of it that stubbornly held on and would not let go. Finally, well after dark, when the only light shining anywhere came from a small nightlight in the kitchen of the cabin, the only sounds from the creatures of the night, Jonathon felt the tears come. Letting them fall, he continued staring at the lake, trying to wring the grief out of himself like a wet rag. Finally, burying his face in a corner of the quilt, he wiped his wet cheeks. At first he thought the grief was for Greg, but when he opened his mouth, the only name that came out was "Fabian."

The cool evening turned into a cold night, eventually driving Jonathon inside and under the quilts that covered his bed. His mind wouldn't stop racing, and eventually Jonathon decided that when he got back to town, he was going to call Fabian and talk, really talk to him. Things couldn't continue as they were, at least not for him. Jonathon had thought that, as time went by, the separation from Fabian would get easier, but it hadn't. Even at school, which gave him plenty of other things to think about, he'd completely zoned out when he was dancing with Karen. Thankfully, it hadn't been long, but all it had taken was that music, and he'd been transported. Finally, Jonathon fell asleep, only to be awakened by the sound of a boat motor.

Thinking, *Too early for Jeana*, Jonathon rolled out of bed, still in his clothes, wiping his eyes as he walked to the door.

"Morning," Winston called from his boat.

"Morning, Winston." Jonathon returned his wave. "Coffee?" Jonathon saw the vigorous nod, and he went inside to put the pot on, hearing the caretaker's footsteps on the porch. "Come on in," Jonathon called from the kitchen, then heard the door open and close. "Everything okay on the lake?"

The pot finished brewing, and Jonathon poured two cups, handing one to his guest. "Yup. Been quiet."

"That's good." Jonathon sipped his coffee and hunted up his workbag, pulling out an envelope. "Before I forget." He handed it to Winston. "Please let me know if it's not enough."

Winston peered inside the envelope, his eyes widening. "It's too much," he said, handing back the envelope.

"No, it's not," Jonathon scolded lightly, handing back the envelope. "You're worth every penny, and I want you to have extra in case it's a heavy winter."

"Thank you," Winston answered with a smile on his face. "Will you be here all weekend?"

"Yes, and I hope to be up at least one more time this fall, but we should be ready to close by early October, if that's okay." It seemed too early to close the cabin for the winter, though he knew that was only because he hadn't used it because he'd been gone for the summer.

"Of course, that's no problem. Just call and I'll make sure everything's ready." Winston finished his coffee, setting the mug on the counter. "Thank you," he said as he walked toward the door.

"Stop by any time," Jonathon called as the screen door banged closed and Winston hurried down to his boat.

Pulling out the bag of doughnuts, wishing he'd offered one to Winston, Jonathon bit into one of the cinnamon-sugared gems, finishing his coffee before putting the bag away. Pulling on a sweatshirt, Jonathon got his fishing gear together and walked to the lake, climbing into the boat and casting off. He motored to the center of the cove in front of the cabin, baiting his hook and casting his line before settling in to wait. Jeana wouldn't be here for hours, and already he was sick of his own company.

When Greg had been alive, this was the place they'd come to get away from the world. It was just the two of them, and coming here was what Greg needed to unwind and what Jonathon needed because he'd have Greg all to himself, for a while, anyway. This was also the place he'd come to grieve, because when he was here, Greg felt so close. Now it was just lonely. Sitting in the boat, Jonathon did his best to concentrate on the fishing line, the water, the trees around the shoreline, anything but the thoughts in his head. "Come on," he actually said aloud to himself. "That's enough of this crap." Pulling in the line, he put his gear in the bottom of the boat and restarted the engine before taking off toward the far side of the lake. The wind and speed seemed to blow away his cloudy thoughts just as the first rays of sunshine broke through the morning fog. Skimming over the water, he let the exhilaration blow away the last of his maudlin feelings. Then he turned around and motored back to the cabin. He'd had enough of sitting around feeling sorry for himself. There were things to be done, and he had a great day to do them.

Mooring the boat, he pulled out his fishing gear, packing everything away before carrying it back to the cabin. Going out the back door, he walked to the small storage shed, carrying his tools to the porch. One of the railings needed repair. He spent the rest of the morning determining what was wrong and deciding a new piece of railing was needed. Cutting a piece of birch, Jonathon fashioned it to fit by hand before drilling the holes and screwing the new railing in place. He was no master carpenter, but his work looked good, and the natural bark would weather beautifully. By spring, he'd hardly be able to tell the piece had been replaced.

Gathering his tools, he placed them back in their box and shut the lid as a motor sounded over the water. Jonathon looked up and saw a small motorboat with two people in it. Paying them no mind, he finished his task and went inside, putting the tools away. Checking his watch, he realized that Jeana could be arriving any time. He glanced toward the water and saw the small boat pull up to his dock. Walking out onto the porch, he saw Jeana step out of the boat before tying it off and Jonathon wondered who was with her as he descended the stairs, meeting her as she walked toward him.

"Dad," she cried excitedly, hugging him.

"Who's your friend? It's obviously not Inge." The figure in the hooded sweatshirt was definitely too large to be Jeana's petite girlfriend.

"Don't you recognize me, Johnny?" the familiar voice replied, pulling off the hood.

Jonathon stared. "Fabian? My God, is it you?"

Hurrying forward, he crashed into the man, holding him breath-squeezingly tight. Releasing him for a second, Jonathon looked into those deep-brown eyes just to make sure it was really him before pulling the man into a bruising kiss. Damn, Fabian tasted good, he thought as he feasted on that mouth, hands clutching lest the man try to get away as he deepened the kiss further, tongue exploring, fingers threading through thick, dark hair.

A small tap on his shoulder brought him back to reality. "Dad, you're giving everyone a show," Jeana teased.

Heart pounding in his ears, Jonathon reluctantly broke the kiss, stepping back but still holding Fabian's hand, not willing to break contact with him completely. "What are you doing here?" Jonathon asked before hastily adding, "Not that I'm complaining." Damn, he was grinning so hard his face hurt, and he didn't care.

Fabian looked to Jeana. "Dad, I'll explain everything inside." She looked toward the boat. "We just need to bring in our things."

Jonathon let Jeana lead them back toward the dock, and they grabbed the suitcases and a cooler, carrying them up to the cabin. "I stopped at Balducci's yesterday," Jeana explained as she pulled containers out of the cooler, setting them on the table while Jonathon watched, arm around Fabian's waist, hardly able to believe the man was standing next to him, his head filling with questions. "I'll finish here, Dad. Would you put the suitcases away?" Jeana was a whirlwind in the tiny kitchen, so Jonathon picked up her suitcase, carrying it to the second bedroom.

"When did you get in?" Jonathon asked, wondering for a second what he should do with Fabian's suitcase before placing it in his room, near the bed.

"Last night. Jeana picked me up at the airport, and we drove here this morning." Fabian stepped close to him, tugging Jonathon to him, cutting off further questions with another kiss that melted Jonathon's socks. With a bounce, Jonathon found himself on the bed, Fabian's weight pressing him into the mattress. Not able to wait for anything, Jonathon cupped Fabian's butt, grinding his hips as Fabian's kisses became more urgent and needy. "I missed you, Johnny," Fabian gasped between kisses. "Missed you very much."

Jonathon didn't answer in words, he simply captured Fabian's mouth again, kissing hard, sliding his hands under Fabian's shirt. Damn, he wanted skin, and he wanted it now.

"Lunch is ready," Jeana called from the other room. "You two can maul each other all you want once we've eaten and I'm out of here!" Jonathon could hear definite amusement in her voice.

Huffing softly against Fabian's skin, Jonathon waited for him to get up before groaning loudly enough to be heard in the other room and getting off the bed. Taking Fabian's hand again, he led them to the table.

"So." Jonathon glared at Jeana. "Do you want to tell me what's going on?"

She smiled at him. "Not really," she said, handing him the container of Waldorf salad, followed by a container of curried chicken salad. Jonathon took a helping of both before passing them to Fabian with a wink and a smile and giving Jeana his best spill-it look.

"I talked to Fabian before I left, and I could see how he felt about you." Jeana set down the bean salad she'd been holding, glaring back at Jonathon. "You've been moping around the house since I got back, and I know you didn't want to talk about it, but I could tell you missed Fabian too. So last week, I called him."

Jonathon felt Fabian's hand on his, warm and comforting. "I missed you too, and Jeana asked me to come. I could not stay away."

"But what about your job? What about Hanna and Oma?" Jonathon felt a little overwhelmed.

"Mutti and Oma are fine. And I have an appointment for a job next week in New York."

"But—" Jonathon sputtered and then stared at his plate. Everything was happening so fast.

"Dad," Jeana interjected, "why don't we finish eating, and then you and Fabian can talk."

Jonathon nodded and tried his best to eat, but the food suddenly went tasteless. He was thrilled to have Fabian here, there was no doubt of that, but everything felt so out of control. He looked at Fabian, saw the worried look in his eyes and sighed. He didn't want Fabian upset; he was just unsure how he felt about all this.

"Excuse me." Fabian set down his fork and pushed away from the table. Jonathon watched as he walked outside and off the porch. He almost got up when he felt Jeana's hand on his arm.

"I know you're upset because of the way I did this, and maybe I should have told you. But the look on your face when you realized who was with me was worth all the money in the world," Jeana said softly. "So think about this. Fabian is here, and he's willing to stay." Jonathon's eyes widened. "The man loves you enough to leave everything behind to be with you. Do you love him enough to accept the gift he's giving you?"

Jonathon thought for a split second before getting up, looking for Fabian. He found him standing by the water's edge, staring out over the lake. "I can go back tomorrow," Fabian said as Jonathon approached.

"Only if that's what you want."

Fabian whirled around. "What do *you* want? I thought you wanted me, but now that I'm here, I am not sure. Was I just a holiday romance?"

Jonathon stepped closer, his hand caressing Fabian's cheek. "Yes, I want you, now and for always. And no, you were not just a holiday romance." Jonathon brought his lips to Fabian's, kissing lightly, hoping he'd respond. "You were much more than that. I just didn't realize what I had until it was gone." Jonathon held Fabian tight. "I love you," he said in his ear, clearly, unequivocally, and without reservation or doubt. The weight in his chest, the last of the anxiety he'd been feeling for weeks, slipped away, and Jonathon smiled against Fabian's shoulder, holding the man tightly as he looked out on the lake, feeling alive, happy, and whole for the first time since Greg's death.

Footsteps crunching the leaves caught Jonathon's attention, and he looked up to see Jeana coming down the path. "I'm going visiting for the afternoon," she explained as she walked past them to the dock. "I'll see you for dinner," she added as she got in the boat, "and I'll let you know how you can thank me later," she said with a grin before starting the motor and untying the rope, the boat slipping out into the lake.

"Do you want to talk?" Fabian asked. Jonathon grinned wickedly, taking Fabian's hand and leading him toward the cabin, up the stairs, inside, and into the bedroom.

"We'll talk." Jonathon closed the door, pressing Fabian against it. "Later." Kissing him hard, Jonathon reacquainted himself with the taste and feel of his lover. "You're not in a hurry, are you?" Jonathon teased as he tugged Fabian toward the bed.

"No, I have all the time in the world." Fabian answered as they tumbled onto the mattress.

Clothes slipped away, lips and tongues reacquainted themselves with the taste and feel of hot skin and hotter mouths. Hands relearned the curves of shoulders and the magic indentation at the base of the neck, the dip at the base of the spine, the slight tickle of a hard bud as it passed under a palm, the special way taut butt cheeks fit and gave under curious fingers. Ears reheard the deep intake of breath when a tongue slid around a nipple, the hiss of desire when lips first closed around a hard length and stopped, teasing for those few seconds, the laughter of a long lick along the ribs, and the near-anguished cry when searing wetness teased tight, puckered skin. Mouths licked hot skin, falling open in silent cries of ecstatic pleasure.

When they were lying curled together on the bed, Fabian's head resting on Jonathon's chest, Fabian asked, "Did you want to talk now?" Fabian's eyes peered up at him mischievously, and Jonathon chuckled as Fabian's hand tickled up his side.

"Later," Jonathon said as he wriggled away before stilling Fabian's hands, bringing their mouths together. "Definitely later." Jonathon checked his watch on the night table. "After all, Jeana will be back in only three hours, and we have so much to do." Rolling over, he kissed Fabian again; talking was definitely overrated.

EPILOGUE

JONATHON stepped out of the boat and onto the dock alone, carrying a box. Looking around the village of Raquette Lake with its general store, single restaurant, and gift shop in a caboose, he remembered the first time he had seen it, years before with Greg, and Jonathon smiled. Things had changed little over that time, and for that, Jonathon was glad. This place always seemed to steady him, and he hoped it never changed.

"Dad!" Jeana's excited voice pulled him out of his thoughts, and he grinned as he saw her close the car door. "We were planning to come to the cabin." Jonathon walked toward her and watched as the rest of the car doors opened. Eric, Adam, and—to his surprise—Doreen, got out of the car. Stopping, they didn't approach, and he wasn't going to force it, but Jeana walked to him, taking the box from his hands and setting it on the boards of the dock before giving him her usual hug. "We would have come to you."

Jonathon shook his head. "I made other arrangements." He tilted his head toward a white-and-red sightseeing boat. "I thought that would be more comfortable." She nodded but said nothing.

Other cars pulled into the small parking area, Marty and Ruthie getting out of one. To Jonathon's surprise, Karen got out of the other. A boat glided alongside the dock, and Jonathon saw Winston get out, dressed in a suit, looking rather dashing.

"Mr. Pfister, we're ready for you," Carol, the woman who managed the sightseeing boat, said softly from behind him. She'd been wonderful and had readily agreed to a private run before the start of the regular tourist season. Jonathon came onboard the sleek, white-and-red vessel, walking into what would normally be the dining area. Sitting at a cloth-covered table, he set the box on the seat beside him and lifted out the urn, setting it near the window. Carol silently took the box away as the others filtered in.

Jonathon stood and greeted everyone, receiving a hug from Marty and a kiss from Ruthie. Winston shook his hand and patted him on the back, and Karen gave him a hug. Doreen stood off to one side, but Adam walked to him, shaking his hand. "Thank you."

"I wouldn't have excluded you," Jonathon explained.

"I know you wouldn't." Adam looked at his mother, who'd taken a seat against the windows on the other side of the boat. "I'm sorry for everything. I can't speak for anyone but myself, but I should have treated you better. You deserved better."

"That past is over and done, Adam. Living there isn't healthy for any of us," Jonathon said with a smile, and Adam nodded, moving away, but Jonathon noticed that he began talking to Marty rather than sitting with his mother. Eric approached and shook his hand as well, but he said nothing other than a polite greeting before moving away. The boat engines revved and they began to pull away from the dock, steadily moving out into the lake.

"Everyone, could I have a moment, please?" Jeana said from the front of the dining area, and conversation died away. "I'm not sure what Jonathon has planned." She looked to him, and Jonathon nodded, relieved that she was going to speak. "But I'd like to ask Adam and Eric to join me." The boys looked at each other and got up, standing next to her. "Today we're saying a final good-bye to our father." Jeana's voice faltered for a second. "He took care of us, loved us, and provided us with opportunities most others don't have. He also taught us and showed us how to love. After he and Mom divorced, he didn't walk away from us or from her. He provided for us and cared for us all." Jonathon saw Jeana look at her mother. "He took us places and spent time with us. When I was in school, a lot of the other kids came from broken homes, and many of them never saw their fathers. Not us. He made time for us and was never selfish. Daddy always seemed to have more money than time, but he was never stingy with either. So, Daddy, I want to tell you, wherever you are… I want to say that I hope you're happy and at peace, because you deserve to be."

Jeana waited a few seconds before taking the seat next to Jonathon, and he put an arm around her shoulder. "Thank you," he whispered before standing up.

"I want to thank you all for coming." He caught Carol's eye, nodding, and she brought out a tray filled with glasses. "This isn't a funeral, but a celebration of Greg's life and the fact that he touched us all, and we are better and our lives are richer for having known him." Jonathon took a glass from the tray, doing his best to keep his voice steady. "To Greg—you are gone, but never forgotten. You're no longer here but live within our hearts. We can't see you, but we know you watch over us." Jonathon lifted his glass and took a sip as everyone else in the room did the same. He heard a few sniffles and saw Marty wipe his eyes. Taking a deep breath, he finished the remainder of the glass and set it on the table. Lifting the urn, he walked through the dining area and out the door to the bow of the boat. He expected others to follow, but he found himself alone. Turning around, he saw Jeana standing at the door, motioning with her hand for him to continue.

Jonathon felt the boat turn under his feet, the wind shifting until it was behind him. Twisting the lid off the urn, he set it aside. "Good-bye, Greg. I'll love you forever," he said aloud, and with tears streaming down his cheeks, he poured the contents into the water.

Setting the now-empty urn aside, Jonathon stood at the bow and let the wind dry his tears, looking at the tree-lined lakeshore. Picking up the urn again, he walked back inside. As he made his way through the dining area, Jonathon handed the urn to Jeana, wiping his eyes one last time, relieved that he was truly able to let Greg go and thankful that he'd been able to carry out his wishes.

Jonathon spent the next hour or so talking to everyone, and even Doreen seemed pleasant. When the boat docked, Jonathon invited everyone to a late lunch in the restaurant, after which everyone began drifting away. After numerous hugs and good-byes, Jonathon found himself standing on the dock with Karen and Winston, waving good-bye as Jeana left with her brothers and mother. "I'm going to go as well," Winston said after shaking his hand.

"Thank you for coming, Winston. Please stop by for coffee tomorrow."

"I will," Winston promised, and he walked down the dock to his boat.

"I should head home too," Karen said as she gave him a hug.

"I can't believe you came all this way. Are you driving home tonight?"

"No. I figure I'll find a small bed and breakfast. I saw one as I passed through, and I'll stay there for the night." She hugged him again before walking to her car. "See you Monday," she called before closing her car door.

Jonathon waved before walking to the boat. Climbing in, he started the motor and unfastened the lines. Turning the boat toward the center of the lake, he opened the throttle and skimmed across the water until he reached the northern edge of the lake, pulling the boat up to his dock. He shut down the motor and tied the lines before stepping out. Hearing the screen door bang closed, he turned and saw Fabian hurrying down the path. Jonathon was engulfed in a hug as he stepped off the dock. "Are you all right?" Fabian asked softly in his ear.

"Yes." Jonathon stepped back, but only slightly. "You know, you could have come too. You didn't have to stay here, like you were some secret."

"No," Fabian answered before kissing him again. "You needed to say good-bye to Greg, and you needed to do it alone." Fabian took his hand and led him up toward the cabin. "I have a surprise for you."

"What kind of surprise?" Jonathon asked, remembering that the last time Fabian had surprised him, he hadn't been able to walk right for two days.

Inside, Fabian led him to their bedroom and unzipped the pocket on the outside of his suitcase, retrieving something and handing it to him. Jonathon opened the passport, smiling. "It came."

"Yes, it is official. I am a US and Austrian citizen." Fabian beamed. Marty had helped Fabian with the paperwork and the official papers needed to prove that his father was Italian-American. "Now I can stay."

"With me," Jonathon added, bringing their lips close together. "Forever."

"Yes, Johnny. You are mine forever," Fabian clarified as he tugged Jonathon into a hug. "I have one more surprise." Fabian backed away. "Stay here," he said as he motioned Jonathon to sit before hurrying from the room, closing the door. Jonathon heard furniture sliding on the floor, and then the door opened. "Come."

Fabian took his hand, leading him to the living room, where all the furniture had been pushed to the walls. Fabian pressed a button on the CD player. "Dance with me."

Strauss's music rang through the cabin as Fabian took his hand, placing the other on Jonathon's waist. Fabian kissed him lightly, and together, they stepped into the waltz.

ANDREW GREY grew up in western Michigan with a father who loved to tell stories and a mother who loved to read them. Since then he has lived throughout the country and traveled throughout the world. He has a master's degree from the University of Wisconsin-Milwaukee and works in information systems for a large corporation. Andrew's hobbies include collecting antiques, gardening, and leaving his dirty dishes anywhere but in the sink (particularly when writing). He considers himself blessed with an accepting family, fantastic friends, and the world's most supportive and loving partner. Andrew currently lives in beautiful historic Carlisle, Pennsylvania.

Visit Andrew's web site at http://www.andrewgreybooks.com and blog at http://andrewgreybooks.livejournal.com/. E-mail him at andrewgrey@comcast.net.

Also by ANDREW GREY

Shared Range

ANDREW GREY

http://www.dreamspinnerpress.com

Also by ANDREW GREY

http://www.dreamspinnerpress.com

Contemporary Romance by ANDREW GREY

http://www.dreamspinnerpress.com

Romantic Fantasy by ANDREW GREY

Children of Bacchus — Andrew Grey

Thursday's Child — Andrew Grey (A Children of Bacchus Story)

Child of Joy — Andrew Grey (A Children of Bacchus Story)

Spring Reassurance — Andrew Grey

http://www.dreamspinnerpress.com

Dreamspinner Press
For more of the
best M/M romance,
visit
Dreamspinner Press
www.dreamspinnerpress.com

Printed in Great Britain
by Amazon